I0623140

THE HOUSE HUSBAND

A holiday story about giving love a second chance

THE HOUSE HUSBAND

A quirky holiday story about giving love a second chance

Shelia E. Bell

Douglasville, Georgia

More Titles by Shelia Bell
Some titles are written under former name of Shelia Lipsey

YA Titles
House of Cars
The Life of Payne
The Lollipop Girl

Novels
Show A Little Love (*out of print*)
Always Now and Forever Love Hurts
Into Each Life
Sinsatiable
What's Blood Got To Do With It?
Only In My Dreams
The House Husband
Cross Road (Coming Fall 2018)

Series Books

Beautiful Ugly
True Beauty (*sequel to Beautiful Ugly*)

My Son's Wife Series
My Son's Wife
My Son's Ex-Wife: The Aftermath
My Son's Next Wife
My Sister My Momma My Wife
My Wife My Baby...And Him
The McCoys of Holy Rock
Dem McCoy Boys
My Brother, My Father...and Me
Book VIII (Coming 2018)

Adverse City Series
The Real Housewives of Adverse City
The Real Housewives of Adverse City 2
The Real Housewives of Adverse City 3 (Coming 2018)

Copyright 2017 © by Shelia E. Bell The House Husband

All rights reserved. No portion of this book may be reproduced mechanically, electronically, or by any other means without prior consent of the publisher, except brief quotes used in reviews.

This is a work of fiction. Any references or similarities to actual events, real people living, or dead, or to real locales are intended are to give the novel a sense of reality. Any similarity in other names, characters, places, and incidents is purely coincidental

ISBN: 978-1-944643-07-2

Library of Congress Cataloging-in-Publication Data is on file.

Cover designed by Shelia E. Bell

His Pen Publishing, LLC
Douglasville, Georgia

Dedication

To those who are in the midst of the tumultuous storms of life!

DO NOT GIVE UP

Hard times are often blessings in disguise. Let go and let life strengthen you. No matter how much it hurts, hold your head up and keep going. This is an important lesson to remember when you're having a rough day, a bad month, or a crappy year. Truth be told, sometimes the hardest lessons to learn are the ones your spirit needs most. Your past was never a mistake if you learned from it. So take all the crazy experiences and lessons and place them in a box labeled "Thank You."

HEARTFELTBOOKS.BLOGSPOT.COM

Chapter One

"You may tell the greatest lies and wear a brilliant disguise, but you can't escape the eyes of the one who sees right through you." Tom Robbins

"I cannot believe you're serious," Susan told her best friend, Ellie.

"I'm dead serious. I told you, my aunt and uncle are coming for the holidays, and they think I've finally found Mr. Right. After Jack's death, they want to know that someone else is in my life and Jack, Jr.'s life too."

"But, come on Ellie. Why can't you just tell them that you've been dating, and when the time is right, the right man will come along?"

"Because, first of all, I haven't been dating and second of all when I told my aunt that I've met someone and we're engaged, I never expected her to tell me that she and my uncle are coming from Dubai for the holidays. I mean I haven't seen them since Jack's funeral.

"Why would you tell them something stupid like that?"

"My aunt stays on my case. Not one time have I talked to her without her asking, "Ellie, have you found someone yet? You know Jack, Jr. needs a father, and you need to love again.""

"Ellie, I agree with your aunt. You do deserve someone to love and respect you for the wonderful person that you are. Jack, Jr. is five years old. He needs guidance and structure and I admit that you give him that, and that's great, but it's just good for a boy to have a good male role model. But, still, you didn't have to go so far as to say you are engaged. What are you going to do?"

"I don't know what I'm going to do. I'll figure something out. But right now, I have to leave. I have a meeting in exactly fifteen minutes with Tucker Adelson the VP of marketing. From what I've heard he's supposedly arrogant and can be a real pain in the butt, the same as he was when we were in high school together. He's supposed to be this super hot bachelor that all the ladies go goo-goo gaga over. I bet he's so full of himself."

"Well, we both know that's not you. You told your aunt that you were engaged when the reality is that you won't let a man near you. You're putting all of your time into that job of yours and Jack, Jr."

"I am not going through this again with you. I'm living my life exactly how I want to. I work hard so that I can make strides in my career. It's one of the reasons I decided to come back to Memphis after Jack died. I couldn't pass up this opportunity. I don't have to travel like I once did when I was in pharmaceutical sales, and that gives me more time to spend with Jack, Jr. Being promoted to director of sales was a blessing. You know me; I want to provide the best life for my son. His father was the love of my life. We'd been together since we were both nineteen years old, but Jack's gone now, and no one will ever be able to replace him...no one," she said sadly.

Ellie studied herself in the door mirror inside her office while she talked to Susan on speakerphone. She wore a black, notched collar, single button jacket like a professional model. The solid white blouse underneath stopped at the top of her breasts and the black straight leg pants rested at her ankles. Her black stilettos added extra height to her five feet four inch demure frame. From looking at her, she appeared much younger than her thirty-three years.

"Look, we'll talk later. Are you still going to be able to pick up Jack from school this afternoon? I'll be a little late today."

"Sure. I think we'll go pick up a pizza so you don't have to worry about dinner."

"You're a life saver," Ellie told Susan. "Love you, bye"

"Bye. Talk to you later. Oh, and knock him dead in that meeting," Susan said and giggled into the phone.

"Bye, girl." Ellie ended the call by walking over to her desk, pushing the speakerphone button to OFF and the call ended. She gathered a file folder, note pad, her favorite pen, and headed to meet Tucker Adelson.

Chapter Two

"We do not find the meaning of life by ourselves alone, we find it with another."
Thomas Merton

Tucker Adelson scanned the growing list of nanny services. It was the third list he'd gone through for the day, and still he had not managed to locate anyone who made him feel comfortable enough to responsibly take care of his two goddaughters. Why was he going through this anyway? How could his cousin entrust him to take care of two kids?

Tucker leaned back in his office chair, nibbled on the end of his favorite ink pen, and perused the list for what seemed like the hundredth time. It was hard enough trying to deal with the tremendous grief that surrounded his heart, soul, and spirit. The death of his cousin and cousin's wife threw him for a loop.

He had been watching a football game late one Monday night when breaking news told about a hundred-car wreck and pile up on Interstate 65 near Alabama. Over two dozen people were injured and there were several fatalities. It wasn't until the following morning, when he was called out of his marketing meeting, that he was given the heart wrenching news that his cousin and his cousin's wife were two of the fatalities. They had been on their way home from an office party given by the company his cousin's wife worked for when the chain reaction accident occurred. Now here Tucker was, four weeks later and he had gone from being an eligible bachelor, and high-ranking executive at a major company, to a thirty-four year old single guy with two children ages three and one.

Tucker, an only child, and his cousin came from a small family. Tucker's parents were among the casualties of the 9-1-1 terrorist attack. Now this, losing his cousin and becoming the legal guardian of his kids was truly a lot to deal with, but he had to stay strong for the little ones while keeping his faith and trust in God to see him through.

"Mr. Adelson, Ellie Cooper is here for your one o'clock," Rosie, his administrative assistant, informed him.

"Will you seat her in the small conference room?"

"I already did."

"Great. I'll be there in about five minutes. Perhaps if I let her sit there and stew for a while, she'll get over herself. I heard that woman is like someone out of a horror story."

Rosie held on to the doorknob of Tucker's office and smiled. She glanced over her shoulder and then came farther into Tucker's office. "Word around the office is that she's all work and no play. Practically every man in this building has been trampled on by her, and that's just for looking at her." Rosie looked around like she was expecting the woman to pounce on her from out of nowhere.

Tucker leaned back in his office chair, and clasped his hands. "She doesn't have to worry about me. I've got the scoop on her and nothing I've heard about her has been positive either, well except that she's supposed to be a savvy businesswoman."

"Who knows, you and her might actually hit it off."

"I'm not looking to hit it off with anyone. I have my hands tied with two kids running around. I can't possibly handle a relationship even if I wanted one."

"Maybe that's exactly what you do need, someone to help you raise those girls."

Tucker smiled his charming smile, stood up, and walked from behind his desk. He reached to his right and grabbed his suit jacket, put it on and walked toward Rosie. "Forty-five minutes tops. If I'm not out, rescue me."

Tucker walked into the conference room and his breath caught in his throat when he saw Ellie Cooper. She was more beautiful than he ever imagined. Her brunette hair was cut in a bob, and her complexion was flawless. He could smell her perfume as he entered the room. It wasn't overpowering, but the scent was just enough to entice him. He cleared his throat and walked further into the room.

"Good afternoon, Mrs. Cooper." He moved over to where she sat and extended his hand.

Ellie gladly accepted the handshake while she tried not to stare into his deep ocean blue eyes that reminded her of her late husband.

As they talked, she couldn't believe that this guy didn't even bother to acknowledge that he knew her from high school. Surely she hadn't changed that much, at least people said she hadn't. She may have been a few pounds thinner—okay a lot thinner than when she was in high school, but she had the same color hair and even her eyeglasses were similar to the ones she wore in school, yet he waltzed into the room like he was God's special gift to women. NOT!

She played right along with him. Since he acted like he didn't remember her then she did the same. The meeting went well and they discussed how their departments would work together to ensure the success of the company while helping to maintain the safety of its products.

During their meeting, Ellie appeared pleasant, smart, engaging, but quite serious. She had many valuable ideas and seemed to gladly and openly welcome his. He believed that they would definitely be able to get along as co-workers. Things would probably be even easier since they worked in different departments across the building from one another.

The meeting was suddenly interrupted by a light knock on the door. Tucker glanced slightly at his smartphone. He had told Rosie to interrupt the meeting if it was still going on after forty-five minutes but they had been in the conference room a little less than half an hour. He could hear the sound of a crying baby and wondered who in the world would be in their office with a hollering kid.

"Come in," Tucker said and Ellie watched as the door cracked open. Both of their eyes loomed large as the slender, attractive, blonde woman walked in looking flustered and red in the face with Rosie behind her, trying to keep her back. She held one kid in her arms and another one was standing beside her with tears running down her cherub shaped face too.

Tucker bounced up from the chair and met the woman and Rosie at the door. "What's going on?" he asked, turning a shade redder himself while Ellie looked totally shocked and in disbelief.

"I can't do this, Tucker. You said you would be gone a couple of hours at the most and hours have passed. I've tried to be here for you during all of this, but I am not your glorified babysitter. I'm supposed to be your girlfriend, but I'm sorry, I don't want kids right now. I'm young, I have too much I want to do, and to be honest, after trying to take care of these two, I don't think I ever will." As if matters couldn't get any worse, the youngest child the woman held suddenly vomited and it went all over the woman's clothes, sending her into a full uproar.

"Oh, God," She screamed and hurriedly passed the

kid over to Tucker while the little girl standing next to her started bawling louder than the youngest one.

"Look, uhhh," Tucker looked around like he was expecting Rosie, Ellie, and his girlfriend to say something to make the situation easier, but no one said a thing. They all appeared to be too shocked at what was going on.

Finally, Ellie jumped up and went over to the little girl. She knelt down to become eye level with her. "Hi, I'm Ellie. What's your name?" she asked the crying child.

The little girl stopped crying momentarily while Ellie soothed her by rubbing on her back in a circular motion. The little girl fell into Ellie's arms and Ellie embraced her. She rubbed the little girl's silky straight hair. "It's going to be all right. Why are you crying?"

The little girl looked over at the woman who introduced herself as Tucker's girlfriend and then she looked at Tucker who had walked over to the coffee station and retrieved some napkins to give to his girlfriend to wipe the vomit off of her.

"I'm out of here," the girlfriend barked. "And, I guess it goes without saying that you don't ever have to call me again." She excused herself promptly and darted out of the conference room.

Chapter Three

*"Never ignore a person who loves and cares for you,
because one day you may realize that you've lost the
moon while counting the stars." Anonymous*

Can you believe the nerve of that guy?" Ellie said to
Susan when she arrived home later that evening after
telling Susan what happened. She munched on pizza that
was left over from Susan and Jack, Jr.'s dinner. She loved
cold pizza.

"It was terrible. Poor babies. And I can't believe he
acted like he'd never seen me before."

"Girl, I've seen people plenty of times who know me but
I don't know who they are so don't crucify the guy because
of that. It's been about fifteen years since high school,
right?"

'Right," responded Ellie.

"I can't tell you how many of my former classmates that
I wouldn't know if I saw them today."

"Ummmph, it is what it is, but what I can't believe is that
he left his kids with his girlfriend like that. Poor girl, you
could tell that she was not the motherly type, and I can't
say I blame her for being upset. I mean how do you leave
kids with someone else for what's supposed to be a couple

of hours and then hours later you still haven't showed up to pick them up or called to check in. What kind of guy is he?"

"A thoughtless one is what he sounds like to me," responded Susan.

Jack appeared. "Mama, do I have to go to bed?" he whined.

"Yes, you do. You have school tomorrow and growing boys need their sleep. I'll be in there to read you a story in just a few minutes, Okay?"

"Okay," the boy said.

"Now, go back to your room and I'll be there shortly."

"Goodnight, honey," Susan said. The little boy turned around and left out of the family room where his mother and Susan were talking. "So, when will your relatives be here?" Susan asked.

"The week of Christmas."

"Oh, well you have a few weeks to break up with this imaginary guy you're supposed to be engaged to," Susan said, laughing.

"Break up? Ummm, I hadn't given that much thought. But anyway, I don't think that would work."

"Why not?" asked Susan.

"Because I just told them that I got engaged and because they're so excited. I would hate to be the bearer of bad news."

"I don't understand why it would make a difference. You're going to have to tell them the truth sooner or later, or lie sooner or later. One or the other."

"Yeah, I know. As usual, you're right, but since I'm not going to tell them that I've broken up with Mr. Imaginary, which one of your parents is single who might want to act as my fiancé for a week?"

"I run a day care center and pre-school, not an escort service or rent-a-parent. Although the idea of rent-a-parent sounds pretty good." Susan laughed again and this time Ellie did too.

"Mommy," Jack, called from his room.

"I'm coming, Jack."

"That's my cue. I'll see you two in the morning. I'm headed upstairs. I have an extra early day tomorrow, and a long one at that." Susan rose from her chair and took her almost empty glass of soda to the kitchen.

The best friends embraced and Susan walked toward the front door of the three-bedroom townhome. "I'll let myself out. You go take care of my boy."

"Thanks and goodnight, Susan."

Ellie watched as Susan walked to the front door, closing it behind her. She listened as she heard the lock turn in the deadbolt before she walked away and headed to her son's room.

After reading to Jack, and tucking him in for the night, she sat on his bed and watched the handsome brown haired boy sleeping. He reminded her so much of his father. It was times like these that she missed Jack tremendously. His death took a huge toll on her and on their son. She watched Jack, Sr., go from being a tall, handsome, and charming man, to a trembling, unable to speak, invalid as he succumbed to the disease of ALS. It had hit him suddenly and in less than a year of his diagnosis, Jack was gone. It was two days before Christmas when he died, which made it even harder to deal with.

Tears formed in Ellie's eyes and she reached out and gently stroked the side of Jack's face. She leaned in and kissed her son on the cheek and slowly stood up and retreated to her bedroom.

Across town, Tucker Adelson was experiencing a far different evening. Things were chaotic starting with his bachelor pad apartment. He had clothes, boxes, and bags everywhere as he prepared for his move. Now that he had two kids, he needed to have a space larger than the 620 square feet space he presently leased. With the help of a co-worker he found out about an upscale, gated community that would actually put him about ten minutes away from his job. That would cut down his commute time by forty-minutes.

"Mrs. Newman, can you come help me one more time?" Tucker called his next-door neighbor, an older lady, while he held his one year old crying goddaughter. His other goddaughter sat in the middle of the floor with a runny nose, playing in a bowl of soup he'd warmed up and smashing up saltine crackers.

He walked through the house, talking to the little girl whose name was Harley, hoping it would calm her down. He imagined that the two toddlers missed their parents. Since they came to live with him they cried almost every day and the oldest one, Harper, would ask when her parents were coming to get her. He could understand to a certain extent because he missed his cousin, Joey, too. The two of them grew up like brothers instead of cousins. When he became an adult and left for college, they didn't see each other as much, and Tucker never returned to his hometown of Talladega except for an occasional holiday, but they talked all the time. They had agreed to take care of each other's kids if anything ever happened to them. Of course, neither of them expected that one of them would actually be placed in such a tough position.

The knock on the door was a welcome relief for Tucker. He went and opened the door and let Mrs. Newman come inside. Immediately, she took Harley into her arms and the little girl stopped crying right away. She spoke soothing words into her ear and went to the kitchen and prepared her a bottle along with some mashed potatoes she warmed in the microwave. She had prepared mashed potatoes, green beans, and chicken nuggets for the kids earlier.

Mrs. Newman walked over to Harper and sat down on the sofa in front of the toddler. She picked her up with her free hand and placed the girl on her lap while she continued holding Harley on her other leg.

"You are going to have to get a wife to help you raise these sweet little darlings," she told Tucker. "Not those gals you're used to messing with who don't have as much sense as these little ones. I'm talking about a woman who has a good head on her shoulders and who knows how to take care of children. When you move to the new place in a few days, God only knows how you're going to cope with raising two little ones. I'll be praying for you, and if there's anything I can do to help you, you know I will. But, you know I don't drive like I used to and neither does my husband. I can watch them sometimes for you from time to time."

"I understand, Mrs. Newman. I appreciate everything you've done to help."

Mrs. Newman helped Tucker get the kids fed, bathed, and down for the night before she left.

"You take care of yourself and those babies, Tucker. You hear me?" she said as he held the front door of his apartment open for her.

"I will. But I have to tell you, this is all new to me. I didn't plan on being a father until after I met Mrs. Right and got married, and that was way on down the line."

"Well, you can't live the bachelor life anymore. You better keep your eyes open and your heart ready and let the right one inside."

"How will I know when I've met the right one?" Tucker asked.

"Oh, believe me. You'll know. Now goodnight. I have to go see about Mr. Newman."

Chapter Four

"Where you used to be there is a hole in the world which I find myself constantly walking around in the daytime and falling in at night." Edna Millay

"Christmas used to be my favorite holiday, my favorite time of year," Ellie told Susan. "Now all it reminds me of is how much I miss Jack. This time three years ago he was dying and it was the most miserable time for our family, but Jack loved Christmas; it was one of the many things we shared in common." Tears swelled in Ellie's eyes as she began to think back on the years of love and happiness she shared with Jack. Out of that love they had one child, Jack, Jr. Jack adored his son, and of course the feelings were reciprocated because Jack, Jr. tried to imitate everything his father did or said. To this day, he still said some of the exact same things Jack, Sr., would say. It made Ellie feel like a part of her husband would forever be with her.

She and Susan went shopping for last minute items for Thanksgiving. She and Jack, Jr., along with Susan and two of the children she cared for in her childcare center tagged along. It made the whole excursion happier and loads of fun.

Ellie had been off work the whole week so it made

Thanksgiving that much more fulfilling for her and Jack.

Tucker sat at home more frustrated than anything. Mrs. Newman and some of his coworkers had invited him and the kids to Thanksgiving dinner. Tucker decided to attend at least one, maybe two. Mrs. Newman encouraged him to get out with the kids so they could begin to bond with him and he could do the same with them. Since he had practically exhausted his little black book of phone numbers, he had very little choice. Most of the women he dated were not the type who wanted to become instant moms. He sat on the edge of his bed and thought back to what Mrs. Newman had told him about knowing when he found the right one.

He made himself get dressed while both kids were taking a nap; something that he rarely was able to make them do at the same time. "Thank God for small miracles," he said out loud.

Tucker made his rounds with the kids and surprisingly all turned out rather well. At both co-workers' homes there were several kids ranging from Harper's age to perhaps nine or ten years old. The kids were fully entertained and appeared to have the time of their lives for the first time since he was awarded their legal guardian by the court. If only he could get one good nanny to care for them, then maybe they could settle into some type of normal routine, something that they were more used to.

He had searched around and still hadn't come upon anyone who fit his requirements. After making Thanksgiving rounds, Tucker made the last stop and that was at Mrs. Newman's house. He ate dessert with her and she had already fixed take-outs for him and the children to eat the next couple of days. He was going to miss her when he moved to the other side of town, but he made a vow to himself and to Mrs. Newman that he would not forget her and that he and the kids would come visit as often as possible. She had a sister who kept kids so on some occasions Tucker would drop off the kids and other times when she was up to it, Mrs. Newman would watch the kids while he went to work. He planned to take Family Medical Leave but he couldn't do that until he finalized a major project he had been working on for several months.

Mrs. Newman was a spry senior woman but she told Tucker that she was not a full-time babysitter. She and Mr. Newman had no children of their own and that was fine by both of them. They both loved children but they opted to spend their years of marriage traveling around the world, seeing things, experiencing all that life and love had to offer. They decided before they ever got married that children for them was not a factor and that they could do so much more without the presence of kids running underfoot.

Now that they had retired from corporate jobs and had traveled extensively, they spent their days volunteering at different facilities or going on cruises.

Tucker put the kids down for bed and settled in himself. He had a long weekend of moving starting bright and early on Black Friday. He was looking forward to moving into the much larger and more convenient space. He even had a childcare center to check out on that side of town that was supposed to be one of the best.

The following morning he was awakened by the cries of Harley and a slap in the face repeatedly by Harper. "Wake up," the little girl said, pulling up the eyelid on his eyes. "Wake up, I want to eat."

Tucker squinted, pulled himself up from out of his bed, and looked at Harper. "Okay, okay," he said. "Let's go see about your sister and then I'll get you two something to eat."

He went into the bedroom that he'd turned into the

girls' room. He hadn't done anything to make it look girly. It remained just as it had except it wasn't deemed the man cave any longer. He did purchase a crib and a twin bed and replaced the leather sofa, his 65-inch television, and other accessories in the room but that was it.

He stumbled sleepily into the bedroom to see about Harley. He took her to the bathroom and ran a warm bath. This was something he had not gotten used to. Bath time was awkward, but it was a task that could not be avoided. He relied heavily on Harper to help with bathing her little sister so he made sure he gave them baths at the same time.

After splashing water and bubbles all over him, squealing, and wiggling, Tucker finished bathing the girls. He got them dressed, including putting a clean, fresh diaper on Harley. Ughh, not being potty trained was a bummer for Tucker. He had ventured off into a whole new arena, but with each day that passed he found himself falling head over heels for the little ones.

By the time they finished breakfast, Tucker heard a knock on his apartment door. He went to the door and opened it to see the moving company men. He ushered them inside and they got to work packing and loading the contents of Tucker's apartment. Shortly after they arrived, his best friend, Bill, came through to lend a hand. He brought along his new bride and she graciously offered to watch the girls while Tucker orchestrated the move.

Hours later, looking back on the empty apartment, he said goodbye to his old way of life and told himself as he closed and locked the door for the last time that his new way of life was in full force.

Chapter Five

"Love is the only two player game in which both players can win." Anonymous

Ellie started her Black Friday before dawn. She took Jack to Susan's day school and she and Susan spent most of the early morning hours cashing in on all sorts of deals. The weather had turned frigid and the forecast called for sleet and snow.

When they were done shopping, Ellie returned to the day school, picked up Jack, and they set out for home with plans to beat the wintry weather. She left Susan with the gifts she'd bought for Jack. She stopped along the way and picked up some snacks and Chinese food for her and Jack just in case they were housebound due to the weather.

"Mommy, look at that big truck," Jack said as they pulled into their private parking garage.

Ellie parked and she and Jack got out the car. Once inside, they stood in the picture window and watched as the moving van slowly drove away. "Looks like we're going to have neighbors," Ellie said to Jack, as they walked back into the garage to get their packages and food items.

A loud booming noise startled Ellie and Jack as they

were cozied up on the sofa watching movies on Netflix. Ellie shook and Jack asked, "Mommy, what was that sound?"

Ellie stood and walked out of the family room and into the front of the townhome where she could see out of the huge picture window. She didn't see anything unusual. She heard the sound again and realized that it must have been coming from something going on next door where she assumed the new neighbors had moved. She went to the front door, opened it, and with arms gathered to shield off the cold, she looked next door. The steps leading up to both townhomes were already displaying a thin sheet of ice and sleet, quite unusual for this time of year in Memphis.

Jack ran up to her and wrapped his arms around her waist. "Honey, go back in there and get your jacket. It's cold out here," she told the boy wrapping her arm around his shoulder. He eased out of her arm and ran and got his jacket. In seconds, he was back and Ellie helped him put each arm inside the light coat. "I was just trying to see where that noise was coming from but I don't see anything."

Just as she turned to close the door, she saw two men exiting down the steps from next door. She saw a man walk onto the front porch holding a small child in his arms. The child had on no jacket to ward off the weather. Another little brown-haired girl ran out and stood beside him, also not dressed for the cold.

Ellie shook her head. "Doesn't make sense," she said. The man suddenly turned in her direction. She almost fell backward into the house when she saw Tucker Adelson. Was he the new neighbor?

The two of them stared at each other; obviously both stunned to see one another. "Tell me you aren't my neighbor," he said.

"You took the words right out of my mouth," Ellie said, folding her arms and turning to enter her townhome.

Thanks for the warm welcome," he said, laughing lightly.

"Don't you think you should be getting them in the house to get warm instead of standing out here making jokes in the cold," she said with a frown.

Tucker looked at the little girl standing next to him and then at the one he held in his arms. He kissed the one in his arms on her forehead and then took hold of the hand of the older girl. "I can't argue against that," he said. "See, you're already a good neighbor." He walked back into the house.

Ellie walked inside her place too. "I cannot believe this," she said aloud.

"What, Mommy?" Jack asked.

"Nothing, honey. I was just thinking out loud. Come on, you ready to finish that movie?"

"Yes," Jack responded and darted off back into the family room. "Come on, Mommy."

Chapter Six

"The heart has its reasons, of which reason knows nothing." Blaise Pascal

Tucker looked around his new digs. The place was amazing. He was glad he'd paid the extra money to have the movers unpack and put everything in its rightful place. That way he could put his full concentration on getting the girls settled.

He played with them most of the day. He considered himself a kid at heart anyway, but he'd never had the responsibility of caring for them. All of this was new, but as he watched them playing he felt honored that his cousin entrusted him to be the guardian of his two most precious gifts. He was going to do all he could to make a good life for them.

He made them a snack consisting of a peanut butter and jelly sandwich for Harper and a half sandwich for Harley. They devoured the food. Afterward, he took them to their newly decorated bedroom and turned on Sprout TV. He put the kids down for their nap without a fuss, making sure he gave Harley her bottle. Turning off the light and closing the door, he went into the family room to make contact with the day school director about the kids.

"Hey, why didn't you tell me that I have a new client who lives next door to you?" Susan asked over the phone.

"What are you talking about?" Ellie replied.

"I'm talking about your old high school buddy and coworker. I'm making a home visit later today. He's a prospective new client, who has two small girls that need a nanny," Susan explained.

"Yes, can you believe my luck? I move all the way back to Memphis from Seattle just to have my old school crush move in next door to me AND he works for the same company. How crazy is that?"

"It's wild," said Susan.

"When I got home I saw a moving van pulling off. Later I saw him on the porch with the girls. Do you know they were dressed like they had been on the beach instead of for this cold weather?"

"Well, I'm on my way over there to see him shortly. I'll stop by after I'm done with my intake."

"I can't wait to hear all about it," Ellie said. "See you soon. And be careful out there. Looks like it's getting nasty," she said and ended the call.

Susan was quite impressed with Tucker Adelson. He was warm, personable, witty, and she could tell that he wanted what was best for his goddaughters. She was also surprised when he talked about his relationship with God and how he wanted to make sure the girls grew up trusting and relying on God in their lives. Hearing the horrible story of the death of their parents and of his was heartbreaking. She understood that he had lived the life of a bachelor and so this was a big adjustment not only for the girls but for his life. She assured him that the day school she operated was a five-star facility and had a waiting list of hundreds of kids.

"You're lucky that you were referred by a husband and wife who happen to be personal friends and their children attended my day school."

"Yes, their kids are teenagers now," Tucker added. "I want to say thank you for agreeing to interview me....and the girls. I know this is asking a lot," he went on to say.

"I consider this as a special request by them. I mean, this is an emergency situation. No one can ever be quite prepared when tragedy strikes," Susan told him.

"Do you think the girls would be a good fit at your school?" Tucker asked as he placed Harley on the floor to toddle around with her sister. The two girls played well together. Harper tried to take care of her little sister. She would try to feed her, give her toys or her binky, and even tried to offer help when Tucker had to change a soiled diaper. Tucker was in awe of the unconditional love the two displayed for each other.

"I think they will," Susan said. "It might be a little tough in the beginning. They've been through a lot."

"Yes, they have. I mean they don't know me. Harper has seen me only a handful of times and Harley is just too young to know who I am. I'm actually scared. I don't want to fail my cousin but I definitely don't want to fail these kids. I'm used to the corporate world and my freedom, you know. All I have to rely on is my faith that God will help me in this situation."

"I understand, but as far as the girls are concerned, they'll be well taken care of at my day school. We also offer evening and overnight care for those times you have a late meeting or a date," Susan smiled.

"That won't be too often. I used to have to do quite a bit of traveling but now I don't have to travel as much, which is cool. I guess it's thinking about what's best for the girls now and not myself."

"You got that right," Susan said and stood up signaling that the intake interview was done. "Well, it was a pleasure to meet you. If you'll get me that other paperwork then we can move forward and the girls should be able to start tomorrow."

"Thanks, Mrs. Loews."

"You're welcome. Did you have any questions for me? Oh, and did you do a full tour of my facility?"

"Yes, I loved it. Quite state of the art. And one of the staff told me about your home services too. I might have to take advantage of that from time to time."

"Yes, I forgot to mention that. We have a roster of certified and bonded staff. If you want someone to come to your home to care for the girls, we can arrange for those services. However, the fee is different. I can't believe I forgot to go over that. Do you mind if I sit back down for just a minute?"

"Of course, it's no problem. I just recalled it myself. I think that they would do well if they attended the day school a couple of days a week and the other days if we can have in home care for them. I won't need it right away because I'll be taking leave from my job for a number of weeks."

Susan sat back down and opened her tote. She looked inside and then pulled out two sheets. "Here is a list of our in home staff, along with their pictures, bios, and hours. You can also log in to our private server and interview them online through video chat. You will need to schedule it. There is also a price list broken down hourly, weekly, monthly. Of course, I'll have to give you an access code if you'd like to video chat."

"This sounds great. I'll read over everything tonight."

"Tomorrow, when you bring the girls, I suggest you stay around an extra hour if possible so you can meet some of our in-home staff, and so the girls will feel more comfortable with you leaving them. I look forward to seeing you and the girls tomorrow. And the fact that you live next door to my best friend and that you two work together, gives you an added bonus." Susan laughed.

"Are you talking about the ice princess?" he shook his head. "Small world. Definitely," he said.

"Uh, ice princess?" Susan frowned.

"Oh, I'm sorry. I didn't mean anything by that. It's just that she seems, well, never mind."

Susan stood back up and prepared to leave once again. "I'll see you tomorrow."

"Good evening, Mrs. Loews."

"Susan, please call me Susan."

And you can call me Tucker. "Good night, Susan."

"Good night, Tucker."

Chapter Seven

"Unconditional love is the greatest gift of all." Sylvia
Masser

"I can tell he is quite nervous about being a father to
those precious little ones. And he should be. He's never
been a father before and he's used to living a carefree life,
you know."

"Whatever. I just feel bad for those girls. I hope he can
give them a good home with lots of love."

"He seems to want to. And he's a man who relies on his
faith. I actually enjoyed our intake session. I think he's a
good guy, Ellie. Heyyyy."

"Hey, what?" said Ellie.

"You should introduce Jack to the girls. I mean he's a
little older than they are, but I bet they would get along
great. Oh, oh, oh, and Tucker could be the guy you're
engaged to."

What did you say?" Ellie looked at Susan like she had
seen a ghost.

"I mean, think about it. He's right next door. Your aunt
and uncle are going to be here for only a week and then
they're off to Florida, right?"

"Yeah, but what you're suggesting is ludicrous. No way would I want him to be my fiancé whether in real life or for the sake of my aunt and uncle. No way! I can't do it. Even if I did entertain the idea, do you think I would suggest it to that arrogant prick. I don't know him like that."

"He's not a bad guy, Ellie. I think you're just bent out of shape because he doesn't remember you. I mean you should just tell him who you are. What's the big deal?"

"It's a real big deal, and I don't want to talk about Tucker Adelson. I need you to help me find someone, anyone to help me pull this off. I only have a few weeks before my aunt and uncle arrive. Christmas will be here before you know it.

Tucker could barely turn in his bed because Harley and Harper shared the bed with him and were gathered right underneath him. Harley woke up crying during the night which in turn woke up Harper. He had placed both of them in his bed and the girls went straight to sleep.

He looked at each of them and smiled. He got up from the bed, stretched as he walked over to the bedroom window and saw at least an inch or two of snow. In the north this would have been no big deal but in Memphis almost everything would be shut down. He called the day school after searching through the packet Susan had left. He was surprised that someone answered the phone and told him that the facility was open as usual.

He got a quick shower while the girls remained asleep. Afterwards he picked them out something to wear on their first day of going into a new environment yet again. He felt like it would be rough on the girls, but after talking to Susan, he believed that she and her staff would do everything to make the girls comfortable. After getting their clothes picked out he went into the kitchen and prepared breakfast for the three of them and made himself a cup of coffee with loads of cream and sugar, one of his vices.

Ellie and Jack were already up and the little boy stood at his mother's bedroom window looking out at the snow. "Can I go outside, Mommy? I want to make a snowman."

"Honey, not now. We have to finish getting ready. We need to eat breakfast and then I'm going to take you to day school with your aunt Susan today. Your school is closed because of the snow," she explained.

"Yayyy," Jack shouted. "I can play in the snow at Aunt Susan's school." He was always excited whenever he went to day school. Susan was like a second mother to him and he enjoyed playing with the other children.

She finished getting dressed and urged Jack to come downstairs with her for breakfast. Sitting at the table, she could easily see outside. Sipping on her coffee and eating a bagel, she saw Tucker appear in her view. He raced down the stairs, looked both ways like he was searching for traffic and then ran back inside. *Umm what was that about?* she thought. The steps had little to no ice on them thanks to a great HOA team. She watched Tucker as he dashed back inside the house. Moments later, she saw his car backing out into the street.

It wasn't much longer when she and Jack struck out. The roads were clear in some spots and quite icy in others but she finally arrived and they went inside Susan's day school. She signed Jack in and turned to leave. She collided full force into none other than Tucker and his girls. "Lady, watch where you're going," he said angrily as the little girl in his arms began to cry.

"Sorry," Ellie said just as angrily. She looked into Tucker's eyes and instead of her anger mounting, she felt her heart soften and her belly filled with butterflies. *Dang,*

why does this guy, of all men make me so nervous?
"Oh, it's you. Good morning, Mr. Adelson."

"Good morning, Miss, uh, what's your name again," he said sarcastically.

Ellie grew furious. *I can't believe him, ughhh.* She rolled her eyes at Tucker and stormed out of the facility, leaving Tucker with a smile of satisfaction on his face. He remained at the facility for another hour like Susan suggested and was quite impressed. Seeing that Ellie Cooper used the same facility made him feel even more at ease. He thought about Ellie as one of the staff members went over the policies, procedures, and gave him another packet of enrollment paperwork to complete for the girls.

Tucker arrived at the office around ten o'clock. He stepped right into his daily routine of phone calls, marketing meetings, and consultations with vendors and perspective clients. Around one o'clock he came out of his office, asked Rosie to order him a couple of sandwiches from the deli across the street, and went down the hall to the office of one of his managers. He discussed several new projects that they were working on and then headed back to his office. That's when he saw her. It was Ellie. She was leaving from the office of Becky, the VP of Sales.

He decided to go for it and he ran up to catch up with Ellie. "Miss Cooper, Ellie," he called.

Ellie turned around. The nerve of this guy. What did he want? After embarrassing her this morning now, he wanted to suddenly remember her name and call her out.

She looked at him briefly, snubbed her nose, and turned to keep walking away. She understood that they were at work and perhaps he had a work related reason for stopping her, but at this moment she didn't care. She didn't want to see him or talk to him.

"Miss Cooper," he called again, catching up with her

just as she was about to punch the elevator button.

"Oh, so you do know my name?" she said, looking at him questioningly, as she punched the button. The elevator door opened right away and she stepped inside.

Tucker jumped on the elevator with her. They both breathed in each other's scents, neither giving way to their attraction toward each other.

"I apologize for this morning. I didn't mean to embarrass you but I couldn't think of anything, let alone anyone's name. I could barely think of mine," he said. "Especially lately."

Ellie smiled.

Tucker was glad to see her beautiful smile. He felt more at ease as he talked to her about the day school, fielding questions and listening for answers. He stepped off the elevator with her and walked next to her as she headed to her office. Both of their stuffy moods and attitudes toward one another had softened greatly by the time they arrived at her office.

"I hope that helps," Ellie said as she folded her arms and stood outside her office door.

"Yes, you've given me some valuable information. Now, I just hope the girls enjoy going to day school. My hands are full trying to go from being just me to a family of three. I'm praying that I'll be able to make them happy."

Ellie looked at him. Tucker looked more handsome and so innocent, yet troubled and full of concern about being in the new position of father. She felt somewhat sorry for him and for the girls, too. She couldn't imagine what the little ones were going through having lost both parents and practically thrown into the arms of a stranger.

"Thanks again, and please accept my apology again for my behavior this morning. I will never make that mistake again. That you can count on," he said and turned to walk off.

"Since we *are* neighbors, if you need me, or should I say if those girls need me, feel free to knock on my door," she offered.

Tucker stopped, shared a comforting smile, nodded, and said, "Thanks, Ellie. I'm almost sure that I'll have to take you up on that offer sooner than you think."

Ellie smiled and disappeared into her office. What was it about Tucker that made her feel like a giddy schoolgirl? She almost told him that she knew him from when they were in high school, but she decided against it. She thought about making dinner one evening and inviting him and the girls over. Then again, she pulled herself back to reality. No way would she ask him to come to her house and never would she think of cooking for him. She shook her head as if trying to regain her composure and began to concentrate on her work at hand.

"Life fails to be perfect, but never fails to be beautiful."
Anonymous

"Yes, sure, Aunt Frances. I'll see you and Uncle Burt in a few days." Ellie paced the floor back and forth. What was she going to do? Why did she have to make up this elaborate lie about being engaged and happily in love? Ugh, what was she thinking?

She called her go-to and poured out her frustration to her bestie. "What if I tell them that we broke up and that he's no longer in my life."

"Uhhh, I think I already made that suggestion, but you seemed to think it wasn't a good idea. So, all I can say to you is that you got yourself into this so you'll have to be the one to get yourself out. You just told the woman that you were about to walk down the aisle and now you're going to wait until she comes and tell her that you're no longer engaged? You've got issues, my friend." Susan sighed into the phone.

"What else can I do?"

"You got me on this one," Susan said. "I have no idea how to help you or what other advice to give."

The remainder of the day was full of chores and relaxing. Jack was in his room playing with his toys and she was in her bedroom curled up on her bed reading a book. The light snow had melted and only small traces could be detected. She got up and decided to make a snack for herself and Jack. She went into her kitchen, made a couple of turkey and cheese sandwiches with chips, a chocolate chip cookie and juice. As she finished the sandwiches, she went to get Jack and stopped when she saw out of her picture window, Tucker and his girls. She stood at the window, out of his line of view, and watched the scene as it unfolded. As she watched him, she wondered why he had parked on the street in front of his house rather than inside his garage. Both girls were screaming like they'd been stuck with a pin. He balanced one in his arms and then leaned down to scoop up the older girl.

Ellie felt bad that the girls were in an uproar. As he took each step toward his townhome, the girls seemed to kick and scream louder.

Ellie couldn't take it anymore. She opened her front door and stepped out on her porch.

"Is there anything I can do?" she offered as Tucker looked absolutely flustered, red in the face, and on the verge of breaking down from the pressure.

"I don't know what to do," he remarked. "I don't know if they're sick, hungry, or just don't like me."

"I just made some lunch. Why don't you bring them over?"

Tucker stopped and looked at the screaming girls. He turned around and went back down the steps and came over to her set of steps.

"Come on inside," she said as she walked back to her front door and opened it wider.

As he arrived on the porch, Ellie reached for one of the

girls. The oldest one grabbed hold to her and held tightly to her neck. The other little girl clawed away from Tucker as she tried to get into Ellie's arms too. Ellie didn't reach for her. Instead she said, "Come on," to Tucker again and they walked inside the house.

Jack came out of his room and stood in the center of the hallway watching the two crying girls.

Ellie led them into the family room. She sat down with Harper and then ushered Tucker to sit down as well. She talked sweetly and softly to the three year old and the little girl began to calm down.

"You can put her down," she told Tucker. "Can she walk?"

"Yes, but not that well," he said and half smiled. He put the girl down on the floor and she rushed out of his arms and over to her big sister and Ellie. Ellie scooped her up and kissed her on the cheek. She comforted the little girls with her words. Jack came over and hugged the girls. He could be such a sweet affectionate little boy. He reminded her so much of Jack, Sr. He had so many ways and features just like his father.

The girls began to calm down. Tucker leaned back into the chair and exhaled. He looked like he was so relieved to have Ellie come to his rescue.

"Are you all right?" Ellie asked him, noticing his frustrated demeanor.

Tucker flung his hands in the air. "I don't know if I can do this anymore? I'm not fit to be anyone's father, let alone two small kids. They've been through so much and now they're stuck with a jerk like me."

Ellie continued to comfort the girls while Jack went to his room and came back with two of his toy trucks. He gave one to Harper and they quickly sat in the floor and played together. Immediately, the littlest girl joined them and the three of them played while she talked to Tucker.

"Come on in the kitchen and I'll make the girls some sandwiches and juice."

'Thanks," he said, rubbing his hair back from off his face. He got up, and looked back at the girls as he walked into the kitchen. The space was open with the kitchen and family room being separated by a huge peninsula island. Tucker could easily sit at the peninsula and watch the girls while Ellie fixed the sandwiches.

"Would you like a turkey sandwich?"

"Sure, if it's no problem."

"No problem at all. When was the last time you ate?"

"Yesterday, at work."

"Tucker, it's Saturday afternoon!"

"I know, but time gets away when you're seeing to two rambunctious, grief-stricken, little girls."

"I can understand. Believe me, and I have only one." She looked out past Tucker and over at the kids who were still playing and having fun with Jack. He was so good with other children. She smiled with love as she watched them while Tucker looked at Ellie in awe. It was almost as if it was his first time seeing her, really seeing her. She was remarkably beautiful, kind, and she seemed to be a good mother. In minutes, she'd gotten the girls to stop crying and sit in the floor and play.

"What would you like on your sandwich?"

"Whatever you have is fine. Mustard, mayo, lettuce, it doesn't' matter."

"I'll put a little of everything on it," she told him. "Would you like coffee, hot chocolate, water, tea?"

"Coffee is fine and a glass of water."

She retrieved the coffee pot from the coffee maker and poured him a cup. She put the cup in front of him along with a spoon, and a decorative container that held various sweeteners and creamer.

Next, she sat the glass of water in front of him and his turkey sandwich with chips that looked like it had been prepared in a sub shop. It looked delicious.

Tucker picked up the sandwich and took a big bite followed by a handful of chips that he stuffed inside his mouth.

"You were hungry, huh?" Ellie laughed as she watched him devour the food.

"Would you like me to make you another one?" She carried a tray of finger size sandwiches and some apple juice boxes over to the kids. She sat it down in the middle of the floor where they were playing and they dashed for the food. Ellie made sure that little Harley got a sandwich. She picked up the little girl but Harley wanted to get back on the floor with her sister and Jack. Ellie put her back down and the little girl stuffed her tiny sandwich in her mouth and picked up another one.

"No, I couldn't," Jack said, responding to Ellie.

"Guess that means you do want another one," she said, laughing and began to make him a couple more sandwiches. I'll make you a couple to take home for later. I have a huge pot of soup too. I'll send you home with some of that for you and the girls."

"Seems as if you aren't as bad as they say, after all," he teased.

"Ohhh, so 'they' have been talking behind my back, huh?"

"Not really, but who cares. I'm sure you've heard a thing or two about me around the office cooler," he remarked.

"How did you ever guess?" she mocked.

The two exchanged more friendly banter, talked a little about work, and then concentrated on the kids while Tucker finished eating.

Tucker and Ellie got on the floor and played with the kids for the next couple of hours. Their playtime was interrupted by the doorbell.

"Keep having fun. I'll be right back." Ellie jumped up and scurried to the door while Tucker watched her.

"Ohhh, looks like everyone is having fun," Susan said as she walked into the house and family room.

"Hello, Susan," Tucker said as he looked up at Susan.

"Hi, Tucker. How are you?"

"I'm good now that your friend here came to my rescue. How are you?"

"I'm good. It's great to see you and the girls having a good time."

"All thanks to my good neighbor," Tucker said as he stood to his feet and looked around Susan for Ellie.

"She's a pretty good girl," Susan said, chuckling. "That's why she's my best friend."

"Certainly," Tucker said. "Well, Ellie, we've taken up most, if not all of your afternoon, so me and the girls are going to go home."

"You don't have to leave on my account," said Susan.

"No, you sure don't," Ellie agreed. Susan practically lives here so there's hardly ever going to be a time that you'll come over here and you won't see her coming or going," said Ellie.

"I think I'm going to go give them a good warm bath and hopefully they'll be out for the night. At least I'm praying that it goes like that," Tucker remarked.

"If you need help, then don't hesitate to call on this one." Susan said, looking over at Ellie.

"I wouldn't dare disturb my neighbor like that," Tucker chuckled. "And she's my coworker too. There's no telling how she'd get back at me if I messed up the rest of her evening."

"Seriously, if you need me, let me give you my number. You can call me. I honestly don't mind helping out. It takes time for adults to grieve, so imagine what those two precious girls are going through. I'll do whatever I can." Ellie gathered the girls' jackets, scarves, and hats. She and Susan put the accessories on the girls.

Ellie disappeared and reappeared with the bag of food for Tucker and the girls.

"Thank you again, Ellie. I promise I'll figure out a way to repay you for this," he said as he held both girls in his arms. He learned in and kissed Ellie on the cheek.

She was taken aback and pleasantly surprised. Susan watched from the sideline at the scene that displayed before her very eyes. She could see what apparently neither of them could see—there was plenty of chemistry between them.

"I'll walk you home," Ellie offered. You can't carry both girls and this bag of food. "Susan, will you..."

"Yes, I've got Jack. Take your time. I need to beat him at this game anyway."

"No, you won't," Jack said.

Susan closed the door and Ellie, Tucker, and the girls made their way to his townhome.

"Come in," he said.

Ellie was pleasantly surprised. His home was beautiful and tastefully decorated. It felt warm, cozy, and inviting inside. She saw an area with toys nestled in the corner and a kid size table and chair set. The house was sparkling clean.

"Your home is beautiful," she said as she continued to look around. "I'm impressed."

"Thank you. It's the same layout as yours." Tucker sat Harley down on the kitchen island and removed her jacket. Ellie quickly walked up, removed Harper from Tucker's arms and stood her on the floor. She bent down next to the little girl and took off her jacket.

"I can do it," Harper said to Ellie.

"Okay, big girl," she said to the little girl and watched her remove her scarf and gloves.

"Come on, let's get you girls ready for a bath," Tucker said. He turned and looked at Ellie. "Thanks again. You've gone above and beyond to help me and the girls today."

"Do you want me to help you with their bath?" she offered.

Tucker looked like he'd won the lottery. "Would you? I mean it's still uncomfortable having to take care of girls, you know."

"I'm sure it is." She took Harper by the hand. "Lead the way," she said.

"Let's do this," he said as he picked up Harley from off the kitchen island and carried her upstairs to their bedroom.

The upstairs was just as decorative as the downstairs. The girls' room was gorgeous, and decorated in various hues of pinks.

Tucker retrieved the girls' pajamas and underclothes. "Come on, Harley. Come on Harper," Ellie said, following Tucker as he walked into the Jack and Jill bathroom connected to the girls' bedroom. He started their water, adding bubble bath to it. The girls jumped with glee when they saw the bubbles. Harper wanted to go back to her room and retrieve toys to put in the bathtub, which meant that Harley was going to follow suit. Everything her big sister did, she wanted to do, which is what most kids did.

Ellie went with Harper to get toys and they returned to the bathroom. Ellie undressed the girls and helped them into the tub while Tucker gladly stepped out.

They both went back into the girls' bedroom. "You don't

know how thankful I am for you coming over and helping me bathe the girls. I feel so awkward when it comes to grooming them but I'm learning."

"You're doing a good job from what I can see. Parenting is not all black and white. You learn as you go and you do the best that you can along the way. Just show them how much you love them and tell them often, too."

"Jack seems to be a well-rounded kid," Tucker complimented. "He must have a good father."

"He did have a great father."

"Did?"

"My husband, Jack's father is deceased. He died three years ago, and yes, Jack is a well-rounded little boy. He misses his dad, of course, and there's nothing I can do to replace his father. I can't teach him how to be a man but I can love him, teach him to have good morals and values and hopefully that will lead him to be the best person he can be in life."

Tucker jumped up and ran into the bathroom when he heard Harley screaming. Ellie took off behind him.

Harley was out of the bathtub. Blood was everywhere. "Oh, my God! What happened?"

"She hit her head," said Harper.

Harley must have hit her head on the tile floor when she got out of the bathtub on her own. It was another hard lesson learned by Tucker. He realized that he couldn't take his eyes off of them for a minute.

"I should have been in here with them," he said as he gathered Harley, dried her off while Ellie did the same for Harper. The wound continued bleeding and they decided a trip to the minor medical center was going to be required.

Ellie called Susan to see if she needed to leave. If so, she would take Jack with her to the minor medical clinic, but Susan reassured her that she and Jack were good.

They were watching a movie in the guestroom that Susan claimed as hers.

"Let's go," Ellie said. I'll drive you there."

"You've done enough," Tucker replied. "I'll manage on my own."

"I'm taking you and that's that. Let's go," she said again and walked with Harper to the kitchen.

Tucker led her to his car and gave her the keys. They secured the girls in their car seats, buckled up themselves, and drove away.

Hours later, they returned home. This time Tucker was behind the wheel. The girls were asleep in their car seats when Tucker pulled into his driveway and stopped. "I'll let you out here. This should save you a few steps. Thank you again, Ellie," he said tenderly. "I know you didn't mean to spend your entire Saturday afternoon, evening, and now night, with me."

"I'm glad I could help. Well, I should say that I'm glad I could help the girls," she rephrased.

"Well, go inside and get you some rest," he said.

He leaned in and surprisingly kissed her on the cheek. She looked at him but then quickly looked away and into the back seat. "They look so peaceful."

"Yeah, they do. Let's just pray they stay asleep when I get them inside."

Ellie smiled. "They're exhausted. They should be out for the night. Go on and pull into the garage and let me help you take them inside and put them to bed."

This time Tucker didn't object. He welcomed the help and it felt equally good to be around Ellie.

They got the girls undressed, put them in their pajamas, and neither of them woke up. Afterwards, Tucker offered Ellie a glass of wine.

"No, it's getting late and I need to go check on my own

kid. Susan tends to let him do whatever he wants when they hang together." Ellie and Tucker chuckled.

"What about a rain check?" he asked.

"Okay," she said. "Goodnight, Tucker."

"Goodnight."

He opened the door, walked her outside, and watched until she disappeared inside.

As he prepared himself for bed by taking a hot shower, he thought of Ellie. She was definitely a special girl and he was blessed to have her living next door. The girls had adapted to her and Jack right away, which was a big plus for him. He wanted them to grow up to be happy girls. That evening, he had a glass of scotch, sat in his man cave, watched a late game, and thought about Ellie and the day they spent together. Albeit, they were together because of the girls, but it was still more enjoyable than he could have imagined. If she didn't work with him and live next door, he would consider asking her to go out.

"There are as many forms of love as there are moments in time." Jane Austen

The following Sunday morning, Ellie slept in late and woke up to an empty house. She figured Susan and Jack had gone to church. She hadn't stepped foot inside a church since she laid her beloved to rest. She never said much about it, but she couldn't see herself inside a church when she felt betrayed by God. She remained angry with God, blaming him for allowing Jack to die. Sure, she was raised up in church and before Jack passed, they were quite active in church and church activities.

Ellie couldn't wrap her mind around the reason that an omnipotent, omnipresent, omniscient God could allow a good, kind, loving man like her Jack to be taken away from his wife and then three-year old child. It was totally unfathomable and she would never forgive Him.

Susan often came over on Sunday mornings to pick up Jack and take him to church. Other times she would spend the night on the weekends and the two of them would get up to go to church, minus Ellie.

She moseyed around, groomed herself, and then went into the kitchen and made herself a cup of coffee and a blueberry bagel. She walked out of the kitchen with her cup of coffee and went to peer out of her front window. A light snow was falling. She went to her bedroom and retrieved her phone. She scrolled until she got to the weather app. The forecast for today called for one to two inches of snow with freezing temperatures through mid-week. It was the first time since she'd moved to Memphis that she'd seen it snow this often.

While she dressed for the day, she thought about the day before. Spending time with Tucker had felt pretty good. It had taken her away from thinking about her life and put her in the shoes of someone else, even though that someone else was Tucker Adelson. She didn't like that she still felt that tug on her heartstrings that she had when they attended high school together. *Get that stuff out of your mind, Ellie Cooper. Tucker Adelson is not the man for you. No man is right now. You're still dealing with Jack's death and you have Jack, Jr., to take care of. You don't have time to get mixed up with some smooth talking, good-looking, successful executive and single dad.*

Her cell phone rang which catapulted her out of her thoughts and back to reality. "Hello."

"Ellie, good morning," Tucker said.

Ellie automatically smiled at hearing his voice. "Good morning. Is everything all right?" she asked. "You sound flustered."

"The girls woke up and they're both crying for their parents. I don't know what to say or do. I know it's still rather early and it is a Sunday morning, so I'm sure you're busy with Jack. I just wanted to know if there was anything you can suggest that I do."

"Be patient and give them plenty of love, Tucker. Talk to them; not like little babies, but in everyday, simple language. Let them know you miss their parents too. Reassure them that you will take care of them, love them, and provide for them. Then distract them by playing with them or taking them out of the house."

"Thanks, Ellie. You're right. I've got to do this, and I will. I'm sorry to disturb you."

"No, it was no bother. No bother at all. Jack and Susan are at church this morning. They should be returning in the next hour or so. Why don't you and the girls come over later this afternoon and have lunch with us. The girls could play with Jack. I'm sure they'd like doing that again," she suggested.

"I'll let you know, and thanks for the invitation. I've gotta go. They're not settling down at all. Talk to you later," he said and ended the call.

Ellie texted Susan. "Susan, if I'm not here when you get out of church, I'm next door helping him w/girls. That's all. Don't read anything else into it. Text or call me. I told him he could bring girls over for lunch later. U r welcome to stay of course (and cook too) ☺

Susan texted back shortly after. "Still in church. Hav fun. Jack is good. I'll bring home food for lunch. Will bring enough for Tucker and the girls. Or do you want to go out later when the church crowd dies down?"

"It's snowing so probably be better to just stay in. I'll reimburse you for whatever you spend."

"Okay. I'll call you when we get outta church."

Ellie changed into a fleece jogging suit, got her scarf and hat and put them on. She fled out of the front door, down the steps, and over to Tucker's house. Just as she was about to ring the doorbell, she realized that she hadn't called the man to let him know she was coming over or to see if he even wanted her help.

She reached inside her coat pocket and pulled out her phone but his front door opened and caught her off guard.

"I'm done!" the tall, lean, brunette woman said. "I don't have time to see to a bunch of crying kids."

She eyed Ellie briefly as she rushed pass her and took off down the steps. At the last step, she almost lost her balance but was able to quickly stop her fall by grabbing on to the brick rail traipsing along the steps. She looked back, rolled her eyes, and said a word or two that displayed her anger and frustration.

Ellie looked at Tucker who stood in the doorway with a sight she had quickly become accustomed to seeing. Harley was in his arms and poor Harper stood next to him with bed head. She was still in her pajamas and the front of them were wet probably from the bowl of cereal and milk that was sloshing around as she made the slightest move.

Poor guy, he looked done.

"So, looks like you've had quite an eventful morning," Ellie stated as they watched the woman jump into a car with the LYFT sign on top of it.

"I'm at a loss for words," Tucker said. His frustration gave way to his signature smile as he focused on Ellie. "You look radiant this morning," he said without thinking.

His compliment took Ellie off guard. She cleared her throat and said, "Thank you. I didn't mean to just barge over here. I thought that you might need a little help. I didn't know you had company."

"Another one bites the dust," he mumbled. "But, I can't tell you how glad I am to see you. I'm sorry that you had to come when you did. I don't want you to get the impression that I'm a love 'em and leave 'em kinda guy," he said. "I'm learning everyday how many women there are out here who do not want any part of a ready-made family. Most of them think I'm lying when I explain that they are not my biological kids."

"There's someone out there who will love you and the girls. It just takes time. If love is what you're looking for then I hope you find it one day."

Tucker looked at her, touched at the advice she'd offered.

Once inside, Ellie followed Tucker to the kitchen which looked totally opposite from the day before. Today it looked more like a disaster area. It appeared that someone had tried to prepare breakfast and from the looks of everything, it was not much of a success. Dirty dishes were on the stove, in the sink and lined on the cabinets. Ellie quickly gathered Harper and Harley while she and Tucker talked. She made sure they finished their breakfast. Next, she cleaned them up and dressed them while Harper cleaned the kitchen and restored it to its original beauty.

"You go to church?" he asked out of nowhere as she re-entered the kitchen and she and the girls watched Tucker sweep the kitchen floor and put the broom away in the pantry.

"Nope. Church and God are no longer welcome in my life."

Tucker walked over to where she and the girls were standing in the kitchen. He walked pass them and headed toward the family room. "Come on, girls. You want to play?"

"Yes," Harper said.

"Yay," said Harley.

"Well, come with me," he said and they did. "You too," he said to Ellie and smiled.

Ellie followed along with the girls.

He spread toys out for the girls and then he and Ellie sat down on the sofa. "So, what's your problem with God?" he bluntly asked.

"I don't have a problem with God. He was my problem but now that I have him out of my life, I'm good." Ellie spoke boldly and with somewhat of an attitude. The subject of

God and religion always put her on edge.

"Sounds like you're really angry. I won't press that issue."

"What about you? How is your relationship with Him?"

"I say me and God have a somewhat cool relationship. I have slacked off going to church since having the girls. I'm not used to getting me and two other people ready to go to church. My girls are usually able to dress themselves," he quipped.

Ellie shook her head. "I guess it's time that I leave. The girls seem content." She stood up, then got down on her knees and kissed each girl on the forehead and told them she would see them later.

"If you still want to bring them over later then the invitation is still open. If not, have a good rest of your day."

She walked gracefully to the front door. Tucker was right beside her and eased ahead of her and opened the front door. "Thanks again, Ellie. We'll see you later," he said. "Oh, I was thinking about going to pick out a Christmas tree. Would you and Jack care to join us? Even Susan can come along."

"I don't do Christmas trees or Christmas. So, thanks but no thanks."

Tucker was speechless. He could tell now that she must have been hurt really bad. He wondered if it had anything to do with Jack's father. Whatever had happened had her totally upset with God.

Tucker described himself as a bachelor, a pretty hip fellow, and women told him he was easy on the eyes. He didn't consider himself conceited but he did have confidence in himself. He tried to treat people right so the women he dated were not ones that he intentionally took advantage of or misused. He dated around and he planned to do so until he met that special woman. It just so happened that though he'd come close he hadn't met anyone that made him want to consider turning in his single guy card....until Ellie Cooper.

Chapter Ten

"What is the opposite of two? A lonely me, a lonely you."
Richard Wilbur

"You should go with him," Susan urged Ellie.

"Why would I go with him when Jack and I don't even celebrate Christmas, at least not in the traditional sense. I give him presents that he knows are from me and not some fictional character with a white beard, big belly, and glasses. He knows I work hard to get him the things he needs and some of the things he wants. I see no need in fooling him. Once Jack died, I'd had enough of all the make believe and all of these senseless holidays like Christmas, Easter...."

"And Thanksgiving. You just so happened to name the holidays that have to do with God and religion. You have to release that bitterness, Ellie. Let it go. God did not take Jack from you and Jack, Jr."

"He allowed it!" Ellie yelled, startling Jack because he ran into the kitchen where his mother and Aunt Susan were.

"Mommy," he ran into the kitchen screaming.

"I'm sorry," said Ellie. "Sweetheart, I didn't mean to frighten you. Me and your Aunt Susan were just talking.

I didn't mean to yell. Go back and finish watching your movie."

Jack turned and ran back out of the kitchen.

"I have nothing else to say. I'm just grateful that you still let me take Jack to church with me."

"That's because I want him to make his own decision about religion and God. For now, if you want to take him with you to church then it's cool. Just don't ask me to go. You know the deal."

'Yes, and that's why I don't hound you about coming. I respect your decision, but I know there was a time that your faith was strong in God. I'm just saying, seeing you with this new belief or should I say *nonbelief* is kinda hard. I mean, think about it. You're the one who introduced me to Jesus Christ."

"I don't want to go there, Susan. Not today. I think me and Jack are going to make a grocery store run. I need to pick up a few items. This snow is steadily coming down and it's supposed to snow on and off and be cold for the rest of week. I need to be prepared just in case school is closed again."

"I'm sure it's going to be closed, but you know I'm open 24/7. I have around the clock on-site staff and they're committed to providing the best care for the kids."

"You're right about that. That's why you have such a long wait list. Tucker doesn't realize just how lucky he is that you made room for those girls."

"Blessed, not lucky, is the word," Susan said.

"Whatever," Ellie replied. "Let's not get into one of your 'come back to Jesus' discussions. I'm not in the mood."

"Suit yourself. I still say it won't hurt to get out of this house. Go with the guy and pick out a tree. Have some fun with someone of the opposite sex for a change. Hey, you know what?"

"What?"

"He will be the perfect guy!" Susan said, talking like she'd just received a revelation.

"Perfect guy for what or should I say for whom?" Ellie asked with curiosity.

"Why can't he act as your fiancé while your relatives are here? I mean, think about it. He lives next door and the kids are already friendly with one another. It's the perfect set up." Susan spoke with a voice full of excitement at the thought.

Ellie waved her off. "I don't think so. And what would I say to the man? He's bound to think I'm coo-coo when I tell him I would like him to act as my fiancé because I told my aunt and uncle that I was engaged and about to be married."

"I think it's harmless. Plus you say he tells you that he has to pay you back for all the help you've been to him and those precious girls. I bet he'd be glad to do it. And it's not like he has to move in with you or anything. Your aunt and uncle will be here one week and I know you two can pull it off for a week."

Ellie got quiet, as if she was actually contemplating the idea. It would solve the problem with her aunt and uncle and the lie she'd weaved about her life. And like Susan said, it would only be for a few days, a week at the most, and third, it's not like they have to see Tucker and his girls everyday. If he could make a couple of appearances over to her place then it should be enough to satisfy her aunt, especially.

"I don't know about it being harmless, Susan. It sounds like a good idea but I just don't know if it would work. Tucker doesn't seem like the kind of guy who would partake in this stupid mess I've gotten myself into."

"You won't know until you ask, and what better day and

time to ask than today? Go with the man and watch him pick out a Christmas tree!"

"That I will not do," Ellie countered. "I just can't."

"Okay, suit yourself. I'm getting out of here. I need to go check on my own house. I'll be at the school later this afternoon if you need me." Susan went and told Jack goodbye and when she returned, she put on her coat, and grabbed her purse.

Ellie kissed her friend on the cheek and hugged her. "Talk to you later."

"When you fall for someone's personality, everything about them becomes beautiful." Anonymous

The following week at work was hectic and neither Tucker or Ellie saw one another other than in passing. Christmas was coming up in three weeks. Coming home every evening, she saw the oversized Christmas tree positioned in Tucker's picture window. She reluctantly recalled times when she was overjoyed when Christmas approached. She would wake up to lots of toys, goodies, and spending time celebrating the birth of Jesus Christ. But all of that was no more.

She couldn't fathom celebrating a God who had no problem taking the life of her soul mate, her lover, her best friend, her son's father. He was everything to her. Their relationship was what she often described as perfect. He made her happy and always kept her laughing. He was a great father and they had planned on having more children. What hurt even more about Jack's death was the fact that she had just told him eight weeks before his death that she was pregnant with their second child. They had gone to the doctor to confirm it and later they went together and were told by ultrasound that they were having a little girl. Sadly, that all came crashing to an end when Jack died. Weeks after she laid him to rest, she woke up late one night, or better early one morning before daybreak to severe belly cramps that radiated down into her genital area. The pain was unbearable. She managed to call a friend who rushed over to Ellie and Jack's house, and got her to the hospital. Unfortunately, the baby didn't survive. That was two major blows to Ellie's heart and spirit. That was it. She was done with God and anything associated with him.

Tucker was exhausted, frustrated, and at his wit's end. Raising two girls, little ones at that, was taking a toll on him. He had lost most of his *special friends* as he called the numerous women he dated and it was all because of Harley and Harper. He wasn't upset with them, not at all, but it was taking plenty of time to get accustomed to his new way of living life. He was used to being carefree, doing what he wanted, when he wanted, with whom he wanted. If he wanted to stay out all night, there was a time he could do that because he had no one to report to. But all of that had changed and combined with his hectic work schedule the new way of life was wearing him out. He was glad of one thing; today would be his last day in the office for a while. He had made arrangements to work from home and to take advantage of his twelve weeks of FMLA because of his new status of 'father'. He was thankful for his position and for the excellent benefits his employer offered.

"Is there anything special you need me to handle while you're away?" Rosie inquired.

"You know how to handle things so I'm not worried," Tucker replied. "And as for anything special, just do what you do. Field my calls and if anything comes up that you think I should know about then you know how to reach me. Of course, I'll be doing a lot from home including the weekly videoconference. I'll be sending you things to do via email, and we'll talk throughout the day."

"I hope you're still coming to the office Christmas party next week," she said.

"I plan to as long as I can get someone to watch the girls."

"Have you signed up on the website I told you about? The one that's similar to Angie's list?" Rosie asked.

"Yes, I've done that. Thanks for that information, too. You're always on top of things," he complimented. "But actually, I've found a top child care facility that offers around the clock child care."

"Is it the one where the girls are attending while you're at work?"

"Yes. I really like them too."

"Well, in case you need the one I recommended, at least you're signed up and from what I've heard, they're a reputable agency and the babysitters they send out are all licensed and bonded and you can request background checks, too."

"Yeah, I read that. I appreciate you, Rosie,"

"Thanks, Mr. Adelson. I hope you and the girls will take these twelve weeks and bond with each other. You can give me a call if you need me after hours. My husband already knows about your situation with the girls. If you need us, he's on board with us helping you out in any way we can. I think our kids will get along well with your girls. They're about the same ages as our girls, you know."

"Oh, cool. We'll have to get together and have one of those play date things."

"That sounds like fun. Mr. Adelson, I sure hope everything works out well with you and the girls. I feel so bad for them."

"Thanks, Rosie. So do I." Tucker gathered some folders

and several other items out of his office before leaving.

On his way out of the office, one of his old flings approached. She was another attractive, leggy, woman. This one's name was Beth and she worked in the same building.

"Hey, good looking," she said and walked up on Tucker. "I've missed you," she said. "You promised to call me but I haven't seen or heard from you in weeks."

"Hi, Beth." He wasn't interested in Beth or any other woman seriously. He loved living the carefree, bachelor, player life, at least he did before the girls came into his life. Lately, he found himself longing for love and companionship. He didn't know if it was because of his new way of life or not. He just knew that he could see himself finally committing to that one special gal, but it wasn't Beth or any of the others.

"So, word is that you have kids now, huh. I heard your kids' mom dropped them off and told you to take care of them."

"Don't believe everything you hear or see, Beth. You should know that. Even salt looks like sugar, you know," Tucker responded as he headed toward the exit.

Beth followed. "I'm on my way to lunch. Why don't you join me?"

"Uh, I don't think so."

While preparing to exit, Ellie sauntered off the elevator headed to lunch, too. She paused when she saw Tucker talking to the beauty queen looking woman. Right away she felt a tinge of jealousy creep up. Why, she didn't understand. She told herself she had no feelings for Tucker and so to be jealous didn't suit her, not at all. She inhaled, exhaled, straightened out her bright wintergreen pencil skirt, and strolled toward the door and out of the building undetected by Tucker.

Chapter Twelve

"He held her like a seashell and listened to her heart."
Unknown

Not having to go to the office was a welcome relief for Tucker. He had one less worry and could stay home and bond with Harley and Harper. He learned how to bathe them, get them to bed on time, make some of their favorite dishes like mac 'n cheese and watched plenty of movies with them. Almost every Sunday he hauled them off to church and they seemed to love it. With each day, the girls began to accept him more. Harper even gave him a kiss and a hug one evening when he was putting them down for bed. It brought tears to his eyes. He felt his heart opening up more and more for the precious lives he'd been left to take care of. Tucker didn't think his life could be this fulfilling but with each passing day he became more grateful for God bestowing him with the charge he'd been given.

While Tucker was at home making memories and bonding with the girls, Ellie was going about her normal routine. She cleaned the house in preparation for her aunt and uncle. They would be arriving a few days before Christmas, which was in about two weeks.

Though they lived next door to each other, Tucker and Ellie didn't infringe on each other's space or time. She saw him periodically when he was leaving or coming home, and if he saw her, they exchanged pleasantries. He hadn't said much of anything to her since extending the invitation to go pick out a Christmas tree.

Ellie and Jack had plans to go check out a movie. As they were pulling out of her garage, she saw Tucker pulling into his driveway. The two waved but this time Tucker stopped and let down his window.

"Hey, there. How's it going?"

"Hey, Tucker. Everything's good. Looks like you and the girls are doing well."

"Yeah, I think so. The best thing I could've done was to take that twelve weeks off work. It's giving us the time we need to learn about each other."

"Good for you. Well, Jack and I are headed to see that new movie. We need to leave now if we don't want to be late," she told him.

"Sure thing. Hey, why don't we get together later with the kids for some hot chocolate and sandwiches. I'll even prepare it," he said, laughing.

"You? I didn't know you were a chef," she teased.

"I'm sure you know that raising kids calls for you to wear many hats," he replied jokingly.

"Yeah, I know that's right. Okay, Jack and I would love to join you, Harley and Harper. Right, Jack?" she said as she tilted her head to look at Jack in the back seat.

"Yes," said Jack. "Can we go, Mommy."

"Sure thing. Okay, we'll see you later," Ellie said and backed out of the driveway while Tucker drove into his garage.

The movie was funny but a little too Christmassy for

Ellie's liking, but she was not about to deprive Jack of the things he liked to do. He loved Christmastime and he was also growing excited about his aunt and uncle's upcoming visit. He didn't know them other than when Ellie video chatted with her aunt. He'd only seen them in person once and that was at his father's funeral.

Back at home, Ellie sat on the sofa reading a book while Jack napped. She thought about what Susan suggested. Maybe it wouldn't be too bad after all if she asked Tucker to pretend they were a couple. She had no other alternatives other than to tell her aunt the truth. Maybe the truth was the best thing.

The phone rang pulling her out of her thoughts. It was Tucker.

"We still on for later this evening?" he asked.

"Sure. What time?"

"How does six work for you?"

"Six is good. Jack is taking a nap. By the time he wakes up, he'll be ready for a second round of getting into whatever he can, plus I'm sure he'll be hungry. The kid has an appetite like an adult," Ellie remarked and laughed into the phone.

Tucker chuckled. "Okay, six it is. See you then."

"Okay. Bye." She threw her cell phone to the side and began to reminisce about her life with Jack, Sr. and how things used to be. She ached for him. She ached for his kiss, his touch and it brought tears to her eyes. She rarely cried since Jack's death because she didn't want Jack, Jr. to see her sad. She tried her best to remain upbeat for his sake.

There was something, however, about this moment. Talking to Tucker made her long for her deceased husband even more. It made her aware of just how alone and lonely she really was. She had her best friend, Susan, as well as other friends who she was extremely thankful for, but no one could replace Jack and she needed desperately to have his presence again in her life, but that was impossible.

She allowed her tears to flow freely since Jack was sleeping. She sobbed loudly and uncontrollably until her eyes were swollen and red. The grief was overwhelming to the point she felt herself becoming nauseated. She got up to go to the bathroom to run some cold water on her face and to get a towel compress, hoping that gesture would take the edge off the ill feeling.

While in the bathroom, her doorbell rang. "Darn, who could that be? Susan has a key," she murmured and hurriedly wiped her face a little more as she surveyed it in the mirror. She placed the towel on the basin and ran to answer the door. She didn't want the doorbell to wake Jack.

She rushed to the door and looked through the small paned window. It was Tucker. What was he doing here?

She slowly opened the door and put on a big fake smile. Tucker wasn't having it. He saw right through her charade.

"Are you okay?" he asked, standing in the cold dressed in a t-shirt and jeans. The weather was cold and she couldn't understand why he would be out without a jacket.

"Yes. Why would you ask that and where are the girls?" she knew that her face still looked horrible from all of her crying and snotting but she tried to play it off.

"May I come in?" he asked.

"Oh, I'm sorry. Sure." She opened the door all the way up and stepped to the side to let Tucker inside. "The girls are actually on a play date with a couple and their children who are members of my church."

"Oh, that's good. I'm glad you're introducing them to people you trust in your inner circle. I'm sure it will help with their adjustment." She smiled slightly. "So, what's up? You need to borrow a cup of sugar?" she tried to joke.

"I'm here to check on you, Ellie." He stepped closer to her. "I'm so sorry you're having a bad day," he said.

"What are you talking about? I'm good. I don't understand." Her furrowed brows revealed her confusion.

"Check your phone."

"My phone?"

She turned and walked into the family room where she'd thrown her cell phone on the sofa where she had been sitting. She picked it up and saw that she hadn't ended her call to Tucker. He must have heard her whole entire meltdown.

She looked up at him. I'm so...sorry," she said. "I feel so embarrassed."

Tucker walked closer to her. "There is no need to apologize for being human. I'm here because I'm concerned. I heard you sobbing and I didn't know what was going on so I came over to check on you."

With eyes about to tear up again because of his concern, she turned away. "I'm good. Really, I am. It's just that some days I miss Jack so badly. Today is one of those times. And this was his favorite time of year. But I'm good. Just having a moment. It was stupid of me not to check my phone to make sure I had ended the call. I honestly thought I did but I guess I just flung it to the side and unconsciously didn't hit the END button. But I'm good now."

He gently turned her around and embraced her, not knowing if she would take offense or not but he did it anyway. She didn't pull back. Just the opposite, she rested in his arms.

Ellie felt safe in Tucker's arms. She closed her eyes and soaked in the gentleness of his embrace as she listened to the steady beat of his heart.

Tucker rubbed her hair and then kissed her on top of her head.

This is what she missed. Jack had left her all alone and she yearned for the touch of a man.

Tucker delicately lifted her face by her chin and the couple gazed into each other's eyes. He saw her tears and used one finger to wipe them as they began to flow.

"It's all right. Release it. You don't have to be embarrassed or ashamed with me, sweet Ellie." His voice was kind, sensitive, and the look in his eyes made her believe every word he said was sincere. "Cry. Lean on me," he whispered softly. "I'm here for you. I'm here."

She couldn't help it; she cried while clinging to him like she never wanted to let him go.

Tucker's heart was breaking at hearing Ellie heartbroken like she was at this moment. He inhaled her sweet scent while holding her. He didn't know when it happened or how it happened but he knew that he felt something special for her. She seemed different than any of the women he'd dated. It wasn't that she was the prettiest, the finest, or anything like that; it was more than that. She'd been given a bad label at work but he believed he understood why. The woman was grieving; she missed her man. He thought about the loss of his parents and his heart went out to her. That loss had changed him forever. That loss was the catalyst for him becoming a wild and crazy bachelor. He didn't want to give his heart to any woman only to have it snatched or broken because of whatever reason, especially death.

He continued holding her and staring into her tear-filled eyes. He didn't know what came over him but he couldn't hold back. He kissed her lightly on the lips.

Ellie didn't realize what had just happened but when she did she didn't pull back or stop Tucker from kissing her deeper and with more passion. She welcomed his kiss, his touch as his hands roamed over her yielding body. She reciprocated by returning his kiss and wrapping her arms around his neck as she stood on her tiptoes. As he ravished her with kisses she heard a moan escape from her lips, and his, as she felt his desire.

When they pulled away from one another, she looked into his eyes but quickly looked away.

Tucker took hold of her chin once again, forcing her to look back at him. "Don't turn away," he whispered. "Look at me. It was a kiss, Ellie. An innocent kiss."

Ellie pushed away, not with force, but enough to escape his arms that felt so heavenly, so right, so good. "We can't do this...I can't do this," she said. "I know you're used to having women at your beck and call, but I'm not going to be one of your conquests." Her words grew more forceful. "You should leave."

"Is that what you really want?"

For a second or two, Ellie remained quiet. "I think it's best." She walked toward the front of the house to the front door with Tucker following.

"I didn't mean to make you uncomfortable," he told her. "I like you, Ellie. I like you a lot, and I don't want to jeopardize the friendship we have."

Ellie folded her arms "Oh, is that what we have? A friendship? I thought we were just two people who happen to work for the same company and who also happen to live next door to one another. I don't look at you as a friend."

Tucker looked wounded but quickly regrouped. "You can't push me away. I'll see you and Jack later this evening," he said, opening the door without looking back and walking away and down the steps.

Ellie quickly closed the door and leaned against it. She brought her fingertips up to her lips, closed her eyes, and savored what had just happened.

"Mommy...," she heard Jack call her name. She opened

her eyes and saw her adorably handsome son who looked the spitting image of his father and she smiled.

"Hey, sweetie. Did you have a good nap?"

Jack nodded.

"Guess what? We're going to go next door and visit Harley and Harper a little later. Would you like that?"

Jack nodded again while rubbing his eyes.

"Would you like a snack until we go over there?"

"Yes," he finally spoke, fully waking up.

"Okay, come on, let's go to the kitchen."

While getting Jack a snack, she thought about the kiss she and Tucker exchanged. Part of her began to feel guilty, as if she was betraying Jack. But Jack was gone forever never to return. Before the ALS fully robbed him of his speech, he told her that he wanted her to meet someone, fall in love, and be happy.

The more she thought about it, the more she tried to make little of the kiss. It was nothing more than a kiss and she shouldn't start reading anything more into it.

The knock on the door made Jack dash out of the kitchen and run to the door. That familiar knock let the both of them know that it was Susan on the other side.

"Hold up, Jack. Look out the window to make sure it's Aunt Susan.

Jack peeped out the window and started calling her name. "Aunt Susan," he said.

"Hi, champ," Susan said to Jack when Ellie opened the door and she walked into the house.

Chapter Thirteen

"Love is a fruit in season at all times, and within reach of every hand." Unknown

Susan was elated when Ellie told her about the kiss. She had been praying long and hard for Ellie to open her heart up again to love.

"It was an innocent kiss," Ellie tried to convince her friend.

"That's how it starts, but from what you said, it sounds a lot deeper. It wasn't a peck on the cheek or lips; it was a full fledge kiss. And I hope you know that what happened is just fine. You didn't betray Jack or his memory." Susan knew her all too well.

"I sure felt like I did."

"Tucker seems to be a great guy. I mean, he has to be. I don't see anyone trusting him to raise their kids if something happened to them, if he wasn't. The staff at the daycare center talk about how concerned he always is about the girls. He's always asking questions and looking for ways to be a better parent...and father to them. I know you say he was a skirt chaser, but how many women have you seen him chasing since the girls arrived?"

"More like how many have I seen storm away from him

since he had the kids?" Ellie countered and smiled.

"That's because they probably want to wear the title of wife; not take over raising someone else's kids."

"Yeah, I guess. Jack and I are supposed to be going over there later this evening so the kids can play. He's going to make hot chocolate and sandwiches."

Susan noticed how Ellie's face seemed to light up as she talked about Tucker Adelson. Another good sign in Susan's mind. Yep, Ellie was beginning to feel again and Susan prayed that Tucker was the right guy.

"That's great. I know you will have a good time. I just stopped by on my way to meet Luke."

Luke was Susan's boyfriend. The two had been seeing each other for the past year and a half. Luke was a great guy and he made Susan happy, something Ellie was glad about. Susan deserved all the happiness in the world. She was a remarkable human being full of love, compassion, and kindness. She adored children although she learned at an early age that she would never be able to give birth to any of her own due to a childhood illness that left her infertile. She invested her time in loving other children and was open to adopting kids if and when she got married.

"Do you think I should take something over to Tucker's?"

"You can if you want to, but you don't have to. He invited you and Jack over so I'm sure he's going to have everything. You could take a bottle of wine for when the kids settle down."

"Yeah, I guess. I do have a couple of bottles."

"Cool, then take the wine and you and Jack have a good time."

Susan said her goodbyes to Jack who always hated to see her leave. "I'll call you later to hear all the juicy details," she said as she put her coat back on and left.

The evening with Tucker and his girls was more than

she could expect. Tucker made the kids hot chocolate with marshmallows and he put on Charlie Brown's Christmas special. He made them grilled cheese toast sandwiches and tomato soup to go along with it.

While the kids watched TV, Tucker and Ellie sat on the sofa and talked. "Are you okay?" he asked.

"Yes. Why do you ask?"

"Just checking. I know you were a little taken aback about what happened between us earlier, but I don't want you to be. You said we weren't friends, but I want us to be friends, Ellie." He reached over and took hold of her hand and Ellie didn't pull away. She looked at him and he looked at her as he kneaded her hands inside his.

"How many other women have sat here and listened to you tell them the same thing?" As soon as the statement came out of her mouth, she regretted saying it. She hated to appear petty or jealous and that's exactly how she was coming off.

"I won't lie because there is no need for me to be anything but honest. I have enjoyed being a bachelor. I love women. I think God made the best gift ever for man when he made woman. However, contrary to what you may think...or what you may have heard, I am not a user or a man who goes from one woman to the next. Do I date...a lot? Yes, at least I used to before the girls came into my life. I am honest and upfront about that with whomever I'm dating. If you've noticed or maybe you haven't, there is not a lot of woman traffic in and out of here. I have wined and dined my fair share, but I'm at the point now where having the girls makes me want to be a better man."

"How so?"

"Well, the fact that I'm raising girls is monumental. I want them to see in me what they should be looking for in a man when they come to the age where they can date or want that special relationship. I want to be a man pleasing unto God. I don't sleep around, Ellie. Never have. Yep, I'm aware of all the talk at work about me being an eligible bachelor and a womanizer. Bachelor part...true. Womanizer...no. I want that special someone especially now that I have these beautiful girls." He looked at the girls sitting in the floor playing, eating, and watching the show with Jack. They looked so happy and content.

"I don't want to pry but may I ask you a question?"

"I guess," Ellie answered

"Do you ever think you'll fall in love again? I don't know much about your past or what happened between you and Jack's father, but you seem a little, well a little evasive and on edge. Like you're afraid to give your heart to someone."

"Is that right?" She fidgeted on the couch, becoming nervous with Tucker's questioning. Was she that transparent?

"It's just the way I perceive you. I may be totally wrong and if I am, sorry."

"Jack's father died around this time three years ago."

"Oh, I'm sorry. I didn't know."

Ellie nodded. "So as you probably can imagine this time of year is especially difficult for me. As far as opening my heart to love, I don't see it. Jack's father was my soulmate, you know. He was everything to me. I can't see myself loving anyone the way I loved him."

"Then maybe you should just try loving someone else the way they need to be loved and not the way that you loved him. After all, we're all different, Ellie. We are unique individuals designed by God to be one of a kind creatures. We need love and as humans with spirits we desire love, but we all need love in our own way. Did you and uh your husband have a relationship with God?"

"Yes, but I don't want to talk about God. He's hurt and

disappointed me enough."

"You've got to let it go, Ellie."

"Who are you to tell me what I have to let go?" she said with a bite to her words.

Jack suddenly looked up, jumped up off the floor, and ran over to where she was and started hugging her. "Don't be sad, Mommy."

"Oh, baby, Mommy's not sad. Now go sit back down and watch the show. Isn't it fun?"

"Yes." Jack ran back and sat down and started back watching the show.

"I'm sorry. I didn't mean to upset you." He released her hand and stood up. "Would you like me to pour you a glass of wine?"

"Sure," she said, suddenly feeling horrible about the way she'd jumped off the handle. She got up and went into the kitchen with him. "I'm sorry about the way I responded," she told him when they entered the kitchen.

"No need to apologize. You may not know this, but both of my parents died during the terrorists attack of 9-1-1. It tore me apart. I didn't think I would be able to ever move forward. I blamed God for allowing the whole thing so I know where you're coming from. But I realized that God doesn't allow anything to happen in our lives without a reason. He will turn our beauty into ashes. Then to lose my cousin, who was also my best friend and his wife, it's been hard too. It made me revisit my anger issues with God when they died and left those two beautiful and precious little girls in there for me to raise. How could a loving God allow their parents to be snatched away? I don't have all the answers, Ellie but I do trust God. I know he makes no mistakes."

"Guess that makes you a better person than me," Ellie said lowly.

Tucker popped the cork, then retrieved two wine glasses from the cabinet and poured each of them a glass of white wine. They stood in the kitchen around the peninsula and sipped on the refreshing taste, momentarily breaking the seriousness of their topic of conversation.

"May I ask you another question? Hopefully this one won't cause any fires to erupt," Tucker said, taking a swallow of his wine and delivering a smile at Ellie.

"Okay, what is it?"

"What are your plans for Chr...ummmm for the holiday?"

"My aunt and uncle are coming from Dubai. They're going to visit with me and Jack for a few days and then head to Colorado to meet up with friends for the remainder of their stay."

"Sounds nice."

Ellie cleared her throat and took a sip of her wine while she stepped out of the kitchen and peeped in on the children to make sure they were behaving. She returned and then responded to Tucker. "I haven't seen them since my husband's death so it will be nice. At least I hope so."

"Sounds like you have reservations about it."

"I do, but it's not because I don't want to see them; I just told them something that, uh, well, anyway it might cause a slight ruffle in their feathers when they discover the truth."

"Ummm, I won't ask what that is. So, do you do any traditional celebrating?"

"In a way. I mean, I get Jack gifts, but of course he knows they come from me, not some jolly old fat guy. And Jack is only five so he doesn't give me flack about a Christmas tree. He just loves the fact that he has surprises as he calls them."

"I see."

"Mommy, I want a tree like Harley and Harper," Jack suddenly burst into the kitchen and said as if he had been prompted.

Tucker chuckled and Ellie frowned. "Honey, you know we don't have trees and things of that sort in our house. We celebrate the holiday in our very own special way, right?"

"Yes, but I want a tree with lights."

"Would you rather have a tree or your special holiday surprise?" Ellie countered.

Jack jumped up and down. "Surprises, surprises," he said just as Harley and Harper appeared.

"Surprises, I want surprises," Harper said while little Harley clapped her tiny, chubby hands.

"Okay, okay, I'll make sure you all get surprises," Ellie said, smiling.

"What do you say we go watch another movie," Tucker suggested and led the kids back into the family room.

With their wine in hand, Tucker and Ellie returned to the family room and sat back down on the sofa. Tucker got up and turned the electric fireplace on to ward off the chill in the room. Almost immediately, it became nice and toasty.

"Ummm, feels good," Ellie said and took another swallow of her wine, which left little remaining in her glass.

"Would you like me to refill your glass?" he asked.

"No thanks, maybe a little later. Tell me, what do you do around the holidays? Do you have any special plans?"

"I'm going to the office Christmas party, I think. That is if I can find someone to watch the girls. Are you planning on attending? It's in a few days, right?"

"Yes, it's Thursday night. Have you spoken to Susan? You know they have around the clock care."

"Yes, but I want someone to come in and watch the girls. I don't want to get them out in this cold if I don't have to. It's supposed to snow again Wednesday through the weekend."

"She has staff that care for children in the home," Ellie told him.

"That's right. I didn't think about that. I'll have to call and check on it. As for Christmas, we'll attend Christmas Eve service and then come home and I'll let them open one of their gifts. I don't have family here so I don't expect company. A family from church invited me to bring the girls over on Christmas Eve. I might do that but then again I want to start making our own traditions."

The more Tucker talked, the more Ellie was intrigued and drawn to him. He was really a nice guy just like Susan said. Contrary to the rumors that circulated about him, he didn't appear at all vain, arrogant, or like a ladies' man. She liked how down to earth he was. He seemed to be a good listener and he was full of compassion *just like Jack was* she suddenly thought.

"Why don't we go together?" he suggested.

"Where? To church? I told you, I don't do the church thing."

"No, I meant to the office Christmas party."

Ellie shook her head. "I don't know. I don't want rumors to start floating around."

"For God's sake, Ellie. We live next door to each other; we work for the same company; so what sense would it make to drive two cars. Hey, you can even be the designated driver." He chuckled.

She gave him a side eye. "What makes you think I want to be the designated driver? Why can't you?"

"So, does that mean we'll go to the party together?"

"Okay, okay. You got me. And you're right; it wouldn't make sense to drive two cars. And if the weather is going to be nasty like forecasted, we might as well go together, but you're driving," she said, and pointed her sculpted nail at him playfully while she took the last swallow of her wine.

They turned their attention toward the children who continued to play and enjoy themselves until Ellie told Tucker it was time that she and Jack leave.

"I'm glad you came over," he said. "We'll definitely have to do this again."

"Next time it'll be at my place," she said. "Come on, Jack. It's time to go, honey." She got up from the sofa.

"Noooo," he said.

"Jack, we'll come back another day. I promise."

Jack ran up to his mother and hugged her around her leg.

Ellie rubbed his hair from off his face. "Oh, I just thought about something."

"What is it?" Tucker asked.

"Susan is going to watch Jack for me so I can go to the Christmas party. Maybe she'll watch the girls too. I don't want to speak for her, but I will run it past her if you want me to and let you know what she says."

"That's perfect. Thanks. Let me get your jackets." He disappeared for a few seconds and returned with their coats. He helped Ellie into hers and then bent down and helped Jack into his before giving the boy a high five. Jack giggled.

"Bye girls," she said but they were oblivious to what was going on. They were busy watching a commercial about toys. She went over and kissed each one and then proceeded to walk out of the family room and toward the front door.

Tucker was right beside her as was Jack. She felt Tucker's hand on the small of her back and it made her feel safe and all fuzzy inside.

"Thanks again for having us over," she told him at the front door "I had a good time and I know Jack did. Jack, honey, say goodnight."

"Nite," the little boy said.

"Goodnight, Tucker. Guess I'll see you Thursday."

Without warning, he leaned in and kissed her on the lips lightly.

She didn't protest but she was still shocked. "What was that for?"

"Because," he replied.

"Because what?"

"Because I like you, and I want to see you again... without the kids," he said tenderly.

She could feel herself turning red as a beet. "Goodnight, Tucker." She took hold of Jack's hand and hurriedly walked out the door, afraid that he might hear the rapid beat of her heart.

Chapter Fourteen

"Love is a stolen kiss, an innocent smile, a passionate embrace." Octavian Paler

The office Christmas party was the same as usual. Someone always ended up drinking way too much and making a spectacle of themselves. Susan had agreed to keep all three of the children overnight at her own house. Both Tucker and Ellie tried to convince her to watch them at one of their houses so she could go home or spend the night with Ellie after the Christmas party, but Susan wouldn't do it. Ellie knew Susan like the back of her hand. Without it being said, she knew that Susan was trying to give Tucker and her the entire night to themselves, but Ellie wasn't expecting anything to happen between the two of them. They were going to go to the party together and then come home to their separate places and that would be that.

On the drive home from the party, she and Tucker talked about the evening and the fun they had. They caught a few eyes when they first walked into the party together but Tucker could care less. As for Ellie, she felt somewhat awkward and went out of her way to explain to those who asked that she and Tucker lived next door to each other and decided to ride together to the party. Just as the weatherman predicted, snow was falling and at first they thought the party would be cancelled but too much time, effort, and money had been put into it and unless it was a blizzard outside, the party would go on.

It felt good to get out and not have to drive on the snow and ice. Ellie was relieved. Tucker was a good driver and maneuvered along the road with them only sliding on the ice one time.

"I hope you enjoyed yourself," he said as he pulled into her driveway after the party ended.

"I did."

"Do you think the girls are okay spending the night with Susan?" he asked with a show of genuine concern in his voice. "Maybe I should go get them."

Ellie smiled.

"Why are you smiling?"

"You're beginning to sound like a real first-time parent. But really, you've only called Susan a hundred times and she's told you every time that the girls are fine. Go get you some rest and a good night's sleep. I'm sure you haven't had that since they came into your life. Right?"

"Yep, you're right about that."

Ellie proceeded to open her door.

"Hold up, I'll get that. Besides, I'm going to walk you to the door."

"No need," she said. I'm good. Gnite, Tucker, and thanks again for suggesting we ride together. This weather is brutal and I sure am glad I didn't have to drive."

"I am too because I think you had one too many drinks."

"Liar," she said, laughing. She unbuckled her seatbelt and Tucker, disregarding what she said, opened his door, got out of his car, dashed around to her side, and opened the door, extending his hand towards her.

Ellie took his hand, stood up, and they started toward the steps. As soon as they got to the foot of the steps, not noticing ice covered by the snow they both fell. Uninjured, except for their egos, they busted out laughing hysterically. Their eyes locked as they stopped laughing. Tucker grabbed her around her waist and in the snow he pulled her toward him and kissed her deeply.

When their lips parted, he helped her stand and walked her up the steps. He waited until she unlocked the door before telling her goodnight.

"Goodnight, Tucker."

"Goodnight, Ellie."

Ellie closed the door and right away the doorbell rang. What did I forget?" she asked herself. She opened the door and Tucker took one step inside, grabbed her around the waist, and pulled her into him again. This time he showed no restraint. His lips smothered hers hungrily while his hands untied the belt on her coat and opened it so he could feel the softness of her body.

There was no turning back this time. Tucker used his hand to shut the door.

"Tucker," Ellie forced herself to say.

"Lock the door," he said huskily.

Ellie didn't say a word. While still kissing her, he pushed her toward the door and she turned the lock. He held her tightly and caressed her face and her neck while devouring her with kisses.

The next morning, Ellie, fuzzy brained, awoke to the smell of coffee brewing. It took her a minute or two to recall that she had not slept alone. Tucker had made love to her through the night and it felt amazing. She felt alive! She pulled the covers off her naked skin and blushed even though she was in the room all alone. She couldn't believe

Chapter Fifteen

*"Love is the only force capable of transforming an enemy
into a friend." M. L. King*

Ellie worked from home Friday. She was glad that she
had the type of job and position where she could simply
call into work and let her assistant know that she would
be working from home. She called Susan after Tucker left
to go change clothes so they could get ready to pick up the
kids.

Susan told her that she would take the kids with her
to day school and she and Tucker could spend the day
together, but Ellie refused.

Tucker called Susan to let her know that he was on
his way to pick up the girls shortly, but Susan convinced
him to do exactly what she had offered Ellie. After some
friendly persuasion, Tucker conceded to let the girls attend
day school and he would pick them up later that afternoon
before the streets got worse. He took a hot shower and
reminisced about the night before and this morning.

He hadn't known Ellie long but it didn't take long for
him to realize that he had fallen in love with her. He had
a couple of married partners who had told him that they

fell in love with their spouses at first sight. Tucker didn't believe it but now he would have to eat those very words because Ellie was the one for him. He didn't think she felt the same way but he was going to do everything he could to convince her that they deserved to give it a try.

He put on a pair of jogging pants and a hoodie with a pair of sneakers and sat down in the kitchen and made himself a cup of coffee and a piece of toast. He didn't have an appetite for anything much because his mind was wrapped up in the past evening's and this morning's events.

His cell phone rang. He jumped up from the stool and ran to get it out of his bedroom.

"Would you like to ride with me to pick up Jack or better yet, I can pick up the girls and bring them home. No need for both of us to get out in this mess," Ellie said.

"I talked to Susan. She's going to take the girls to day school and I'm going to pick them up from there later this afternoon. She said you were going to do the same."

Ellie smiled over the phone. That was Susan for her, but she loved her best friend for reasons just like this. Susan wanted her happy and she understood that, but Susan also had her own life to live, and Ellie didn't want to infringe upon that. She and Luke should be spending time together themselves, but Susan had a tendency to put others needs before her own.

"I told her I was coming to pick up Jack."

"Like I said, that's not what she told me but let me know what you're going to do. If you're adamant about going to get him then I'll call Susan back and tell her that I'm going to pick up the girls too."

"No, never mind. I'll call her. I guess her taking him to day school would be cool. It is closer to where we live."

"Okay, then it's settled."

"What's settled?" Ellie asked.

"We have the whole day to spend together," Tucker said.

There was no denying it, Ellie wasn't going to be able to resist the charms of Tucker Adelson. She thought about her husband, and just for a moment she felt guilt trying to rear its ugly head, but then Jack's voice seemed to speak into her ear. *It's okay. It's time to move forward, Ellie.*

"Why don't you come over here? I'm sure we'll figure out what to do when you get here," he said flirtatiously.

"Okay. I'll be over soon."

Ellie dressed and scurried off to Tucker's place. He greeted her with a kiss as soon as he opened the door. They had a repeat performance of the night before and this morning. Laying in each other's arms in his king bed, they talked.

"When did you say your aunt and uncle are going to be here?"

"Next week."

"Do you need to do anything in preparation for them? Because if you do, now is the time. I can take you around while we don't have the kids to worry about."

"I have to make preparations all right. Just not the kind that warrants you taking me around." She blushed.

Tucker turned to face her without letting her go. "What do you mean by that?" he asked. "Is it anything I can help you with?"

She laughed and before she knew it, she had blurted out the whole story of what she'd told her aunt and uncle about being engaged.

Tucker sat up in the bed and looked down at her. He smoothed the hair back from her face, kissed her lips, and said, "Ellie Cooper, meet your house husband." He laughed while Ellie looked confused.

"Huh, house husband? What are you talking about?"

"I'll be the guy, your soulmate, your future husband.

Whatever it takes to make your aunt satisfied that her one and only niece is happy and doing well, then we'll do it. I'll be the house husband since I *am* off work for the next ten weeks. I'll take care of the kids while you bring home the bacon," he said, laughing even harder.

Ellie looked at him like he was a crazy person. "You're serious aren't you?"

"Dead serious," he said, trying to remove the smile from his handsome face so he could convince her that he was indeed for real.

"Why?"

"Why what?"

"Why are you willing to do something like that for me?"

Tucker grew serious. He kissed her and then looked deep into her soft green eyes. "Because, I've fallen for you, Ellie Cooper. I know you may think it sounds crazy, but it's the truth. I'm in love with you. I think I fell for you the first time I saw you at the office. I didn't want to accept it and I didn't trust what my heart was telling me."

"What changed?" she said. "If you didn't trust your heart then what makes you say you love me. I...I'm not sure I know what to say or do."

"You don't have to say or do anything. I know you probably don't feel the same way about me....at least...not yet. But I'm going to do everything I can to make you love me."

"Do you know how crazy I was about you?"

"Huh?" he looked totally confused.

"You don't remember do you?"

"Remember what? What are you talking about, Ellie?"

"In high school. I had the biggest crush on you but you wouldn't give me the time of day. Oh, well you did ask me out one time but you stood me up to go out with Izzy McDaniels, the most popular girl in the school."

"We went to the same high school? Noooo, I...I would have remembered. Are you sure it was me?"

"Oh, believe me it was you, and yes, we attended the same high school. I didn't know if you actually didn't remember me for real or if you were just being an arrogant prick like you used to be in high school."

"Ellie? I don't remember Ellie in high school."

"That's because in high school everyone called me by my real name, Ellisandra."

"What? You're Ellisandra Reynolds? No way," Tucker said, appearing shocked.

"The one and only. I was much heavier back then and had a face full of acne but you still asked me out. I don't think you were serious then and I don't know if you're serious now. I know we've slept together and that's my fault. I shouldn't have crossed the line. I...I'm sorry. I better leave." Ellie said, suddenly having second thoughts about everything that had happened and that was unfolding before her. She made a move to get up out of his bed, but Tucker stopped her.

"Where are you going?"

"Home. This isn't right. You know it and I know it. It's no use in us starting something that we both know isn't going to work."

"I just told you that I'm in love with you, Ellie. I'm sorry that I didn't recognize you, but you look like a totally different person and your name, all of that well I just didn't remember. But I can tell you what I do remember. I remember back in high school that I had the biggest crush on you too. I wanted to take you out but the guys on the football team egged me on to ask Izzy out. She had been riding my jock for the longest, asking me to take her out so I gave in. I felt horrible because when we went out all I could think about was you and how I had hurt you. I pretended like it didn't bother me and you know, after that I tried to say something to you, but you wouldn't have anything else to do with me and I couldn't blame you. I was a real jerk."

Ellie looked at him in unbelief. She didn't know if he was telling her the truth or feeding her empty words, but she wanted to believe him. He sounded sincere, he looked sincere, but was he or had he made the whole thing up?"

"I...I don't know what to say. I don't know if I can believe you, Tucker."

"You can believe me, Ellisandra." He gathered her in his arms and began kissing her face, her hair, her neck, and her soft lips. He devoured her body with his hands as he whispered hoarsely, "I love you, Ellie. Believe me, please. And I want you to love me too. Let me prove it to you."

Ellie gave in to her flesh and her heart. She ached for him and only he could fulfill her desire. The past was in the past. She had to learn to leave the past behind. After all, they were kids back then. She didn't remember half the people she went to school with so why would she expect him to remember her.

So, Ellie Cooper, will you allow me to be your house husband?" he teased after their latest round of making love while they were in the shower.

The warm jets of water cascaded down their bodies and Tucker washed her with his soapy hands. Ellie could barely contain herself. "How can I say no if you're going to be doing things like this," she was barely able to respond.

"That's the point. I don't want you to say no. I want you. All of you. I'll be the perfect fiancé when your aunt and uncle come."

Chapter Sixteen

"I need you like a heart needs a beat." Unknown

The next two weeks were magical and Ellie couldn't be happier. She and Tucker were together every day. When she got home from work she and Jack would either hang out at Tucker's house or Tucker and the girls would be at her house.

The day arrived when she had to pick up her aunt and uncle from the airport. Part of her was excited and the other part of her was nervous because she didn't know how things would work out with the lie she'd concocted.

Without incident, she picked up her relatives and they greeted and hugged one another. She had no idea she would break out in tears when she saw them but she did. It was a bit overwhelming for her because her aunt reminded her so much of her deceased mother, to the point that the similarities in their resemblance was uncanny.

"Where is your fiancé'? I thought he would have come along with you and Jack," her aunt told her, full of excitement that her niece was finally going to be happy again.

"You'll meet him soon enough," Ellie replied.

Upon arriving at the townhome, they all walked inside and were met with the aroma of food, good smelling food.

Ellie assumed Susan had come and prepared something to eat, which was not unusual for Susan to do. A few steps inside and Susan appeared.

"Hey, girl," Ellie said. "I'd like you to meet my aunt and uncle."

They all exchanged pleasantries and then Ellie remarked, "You sure have it smelling good up in here."

"Uh, I wish I could take the credit but it wasn't me," Susan responded and looked over her shoulder, and that's when Tucker appeared.

"Hello," he said, coming into the foyer with a giant smile on his handsome face and wearing an apron. "Sooo, this is my soon to be aunt and uncle." He walked up to Ellie's aunt, hugged her, and then turned and shook the uncle's hand. Next, he walked up and positioned himself next to Ellie and Jack. He wrapped his arm around Ellie's petite waist and kissed her on the temple. "I'm Tucker...Tucker Adelson. Ellie has told me so much about you. She's been on pins and needles ever since you guys told her you were coming."

"It is certainly nice to meet you," her aunt said, looking totally pleased. Her uncle spoke as well, and also seemed pleased.

"I hope you guys are hungry. I'm not the world's best cook, but I prepared a little something for you. It's actually one of Jack's favorite meals. Mac 'n cheese, baked chicken, and green beans."

"Yayyy," said Jack.

"Impressive," Ellie's aunt said while Ellie herself smiled in total surprise. She almost burst out laughing seeing Tucker dressed in a full apron like he was an iron chef and it was hilarious to see, but it also made Ellie feel proud. Tucker had gone all out to make a good first impression.

"Who are these precious little ones?" her uncle asked

as the girls appeared.

Tucker introduced the girls then turned and looked down at Jack. "Jack, what do you say we go outside, get the luggage, and bring it inside. You think you're up for the challenge? You think you're strong enough?"

"Yes, I'm real strong. I'm strong like Spiderman," he said, sounding proud, and making a stance like he'd seen Spiderman do on the movie.

"We'll be right back," he told Ellie and the others.

"This food is delicious," Ellie's aunt complimented and her uncle agreed. Susan smiled at Ellie and nodded like she was giving her a blessing or something. Tucker squeezed Ellie's thigh underneath the dining room table.

Later that evening they gathered in the family room. Susan had left and Ellie was left alone with her relatives, the kids, and Tucker.

"So what are the plans for Christmas? I'd love to go to church. Tucker, do you go to church?" her aunt asked, making Ellie feel a little uneasy.

"Yes, I do. My church is having Christmas Eve service. I would love it if you would accompany us."

"Of course, we would love to. Right, honey?" the aunt said and turned to her husband for his agreement. He nodded.

"Ellie, what about you? I hope you'll consider going with us. I know your feelings about God and church, but this is not about church. This is about family. And you should take the lead of your soon to be husband if you want this relationship...and marriage to work."

Ellie said very little, only that she would think about going.

The next couple of days went by like a whirlwind. Ellie's

aunt took to Tucker. Ellie had taken off work until after the new year. The weather had cleared so she and her aunt spent time shopping for gifts for Jack and Tucker's girls.

"I think Tucker is absolutely amazing," her aunt told her as they had lunch at one of the restaurants in the food court of the mall.

"Yes, he is a good guy," Ellie remarked. With each passing day she was falling more in love with Tucker Adelson. She didn't know exactly when it happened or how it happened, but she had made up in her mind that she wasn't going to fight her feelings any longer. She had a dream a few nights ago where her husband appeared. He was telling her that it was time for her to move on with her life and that he was fine and happy. She woke up unsure if it was a dream or if Jack had actually visited her in spirit. A feeling of calm and serene peace filled her and she smiled because she felt that she had been given his blessing.

"So, when is the wedding? I hope me and your uncle can come back to the States to attend."

"It won't be right away. I mean so much has been going on at work and I have a lot of things on my plate. Planning a wedding takes time, you know."

"Yes, I know, but you don't have to have anything elaborate. You can do a small wedding with a few friends and then have a large reception," her aunt suggested.

"Yes, I guess you're right. Do you have any more stores you want to stop at?" Ellie asked, trying to get her aunt off the subject of marriage.

"Maybe a couple more. It is Christmas Eve and the stores are closing early so let's finish eating and get the rest of the shopping done," she said.

The ladies shopped until they dropped. At home, Tucker and Ellie's uncle were watching a game while the kids played.

what she had allowed to happen.

Tucker was sensitive, an expert lover, and he made her feel like she was the most special girl in the world. She got up from the bed and was about to grab her robe from off the nearby chair.

"Good morning, sleepy head," Tucker said, suddenly appearing in the bedroom with a tray of food and dressed only in his bottoms. This time she was truly embarrassed because there she stood at the side of the bed in nothing but her bare skin. She quickly used both hands to cover her breasts and private parts.

Tucker smiled. "I've seen it....and touched it all."

She turned crimson but still grabbed her robe and put it on. "What's this?" she asked, eyeing the tray.

"Breakfast. Now get back in the bed, madam, and let me serve you."

At first Ellie was reluctant, but she climbed back in the bed without removing her robe.

Tucker walked over with a tray of food that held bacon, eggs, toast, orange juice, and coffee." It looked divine.

"I hope you like it. I didn't know how you liked your eggs or your coffee."

"I can't believe you found your way around in my kitchen," she said. "This looks delicious. Thank you."

He sat the tray on the nightstand next to the bed and then kissed her. When their lips parted he got the tray of food and sat it on her lap. He picked up the fork and got a piece of scrambled egg and bacon and fed it to her.

"Ummm, this is delicious," she said. "Where is your food?"

"Believe me, I have all that I need or want right here in front of me."

That evening, Tucker went home and got ready for church. Ellie came over to talk to him.

"I don't think I can do this," she said. "I haven't been inside a church since...well, you know."

Tucker held her in his arms and stared down at her. "I'm not going to force you. This has to be something you make a decision about on your own. Just know that I love you, Ellie. I want us to do everything together and that includes us both having a relationship with God. But I can't make that decision for you. It has to come from you."

"Yeah, I know. I'll try. I mean, it's only for a couple of hours at the most and it'll make my aunt and uncle happy."

"And it'll make me happy, too," Tucker said and kissed her deeply.

Chapter Seventeen

"We cannot start over, but we can begin now and make a new beginning." Unknown

At home, Ellie went to her room and thought about what she would do. She felt a nudge in her spirit, like a voice, telling her that she should go with them to the Christmas Eve service. She showered and got dressed just as she heard her aunt welcoming Tucker inside.

"She's in her room. I don't think she's going," she heard her aunt tell Tucker.

"I hope you aren't too disappointed that you'll have to hang with me then," Tucker teased.

Ellie heard her aunt's laughter. She opened the door of her bedroom, sighed, and then walked out of the room and into the family room where everyone had gathered. Her aunt was putting on her coat.

Tucker's breath caught in his throat when he saw Ellie appear. She looked radiant and at that moment he wanted to run up to her and squeeze her tightly, but he restrained himself. Instead he said, "You look beautiful."

"You're going with us?" her aunt asked, looking exceptionally pleased.

"Uhh, yes. I mean, what can two hours hurt?" Ellie said. "Let's do this."

Once inside the church, Ellie was pleasantly surprised at the love and admiration the people seemed to have for Tucker and the girls. Several people walked up to him, hugging him, and greeting him. Tucker introduced Ellie and her family and they readily greeted them with a show of love by hugging them and welcoming them too.

"We are here to celebrate the birth of our Lord and Savior Jesus Christ. It's a time of year where gifts are given, children expectantly wait for Santa, and families come together to celebrate the biggest holiday of the year. But I want to tell you that it's more to it than physical presents, gathering of family, and eating stuffing and turkey. It's about giving. How much are you giving?" the pastor said. "How much are you holding back? Some of you this evening are holding on to the past and what you believe should have happened or could have happened."

Initially, Ellie felt strange and awkward being inside an actual church after all these years, but as she listened to the pastor, her heart and spirit began to thirst for his words. They felt like a soothing salve and she felt herself being transformed right there in the church.

"It's time to let go of whatever it is that's keeping you from giving your best gifts, the best of you. It's time to ask God on this day to restore what was stolen from you. It's time to not only celebrate His birth but celebrate the new birth you can have in Him."

Ellie couldn't hold back, tears began to flow from her eyes. Tucker looked at her and grabbed hold of her hand. He squeezed it, and tenderly massaged it inside of his.

On the other side, Ellie's aunt reached inside her purse and pulled out some tissue and put it in her other hand, then patted her on the thigh.

"God allows many things in our lives and in the lives of our loved ones that we may not always understand," the pastor said as if he was talking directly to Ellie. "But now is not the time to turn away from Jesus Christ. I guarantee this, if He allowed it to happen, He will make that thing or situation work out for your good. You may not see it, may not feel it, may not understand it, but I'm telling you that He will always prove himself to you and to me. So, as we prepare to celebrate His birth, I ask you to release the anger and usher in the peace of the son of God."

At the end of the service, the pastor extended an invitation to any and every one to come forward for prayer or to make a commitment to Christ.

Ellie couldn't contain herself. She stood up, eased pass her aunt and slowly took the walk to the front of the church. Tucker got up and walked with her, taking hold of her hand as she walked up the aisle.

At the altar, they kneeled and a minister came over and prayed with her. Ellie felt a release in her spirit. She hadn't felt peace like this since before Jack's death. But tonight she knew that she was back in the place where she belonged. She glanced up and over at Tucker who had his arm around her shoulder and had closed eyes and a bowed head. She did love him and she wanted to have a new start.

When she got up they walked back to the pew. She was still crying softly. Her aunt embraced her as she sat down.

Back at Tucker's place, the family gathered for a late snack. "Excuse me," Ellie said as they laughed and made small talk while eating. "I want to say something, please."

The adults stopped and focused on Ellie. She looked so fragile, so frightened, yet she stood with a stance that said a change had occurred in her life. Tucker looked lovingly at the woman he had fallen in love with. He wanted to erase all of her hurt, her pain, her heartache, but he knew that it was not in his power to erase the past or what had happened.

"I want to thank you, aunt and uncle for coming to spend the holiday with me and Jack, but I need to come clean about something," she said, looking at Tucker briefly and then averting her eyes to her aunt. "I've lied to you."

Her aunt frowned slightly in curiosity more than anger.

"Lied about what?" her aunt asked.

Ellie revealed the truth about her and Tucker and that the two of them weren't engaged at all, and never had been. She told them about how she had come up with the elaborate lie only to get her aunt from constantly telling her that she needed to move on with life after Jack.

"It's been a difficult three years without him. Jack was the light of my life. After he died I never planned to love again or open my heart again. Then something happened or should I say *someone* happened. Tucker came into my life...and Jack's." She looked lovingly at Tucker with tears forming in the crest of her eyes. "I prejudged him initially but he's turned out to be the one God used to penetrate my wall of defense." Ellie looked at Tucker and smiled. He reached up and took hold of her hand as she stood next to him. "I know I was wrong to lie to you, and for that I'm sorry. Tucker. I apologize to you, too. You see, Tucker stepped in and acted like we were engaged so I could save face with you, aunt and uncle. He did it for me as a friend to protect me. I hope all of you will forgive me."

"Oh, honey, there's nothing to forgive," her aunt told her. "Not on me and your uncle's part. But what I'm seeing between you and Tucker is more than just someone who stepped in as a friend. This man loves you and whether you can see it or not, you love him, too. There's no denying that. Am I right?" she asked, looking at Ellie and then Tucker.

Tucker and Ellie both nodded. Ellie nodded through

tears that flowed. Tucker stood up and this time he took her into his arms. "Everything is going to be okay, Ellie. You don't owe me an apology. Your aunt is right. I love you, Ellisandra Cooper."

"And I love you, Tucker Adelson." The couple kissed.

"Why are you kissing my mama?" Jack said.

"Because I love her," Tucker replied. "Is that all right with you?"

"Yes," said Jack and then continued eating without missing a beat.

Christmas was celebrated at Tucker's. They gathered in his family room around the tree and watched the children unwrap their gifts. Life was turning out to be good and Tucker couldn't be happier.

Ellie gave her aunt and uncle their gifts and they did the same. When it came to Tucker, she passed him his gift. He opened it and loved the shirt, sweater and of all things a red chef's apron with the words "House Husband" embroidered on it.

"I love it." Tucker laughed. "Thank you, babe," he said, kissing her on the cheek. "And here's my gift to you," he said.

Ellie waited and looked around but Tucker didn't give her anything. "Where is it? What is it?" she asked. "Is it a BMW," she said, laughing and pretending to go walk toward the window.

Tucker took hold of her hand. "No, it's not a BMW," he said.

Taking her by total surprise he said, "I know by everyday standards we haven't known each other long, well we have but we haven't," he said, sounding a tad bit confused. "What I'm trying to say is that I love you, Ellie. I know some may say all of this is happening too fast, but

I don't care. My heart knows what it wants and it wants you...and it wants Jack. When I lost my parents, and then my cousin and his wife died, I realized how precious, short and unpredictable life can be. This moment is all we have and even it is fleeting."

Ellie's uncle nodded. Ellie looked at Tucker with tears in her eyes. She whispered, "I love you, too, Tucker." She reached out to embrace him, but he stopped her by dropping down to one knee.

Ellie placed her hand over her mouth and gasped. Her aunt, said, "Lord, have mercy. Thank you, God."

"Ellisandra Cooper...and come over here, Jack." Jack ran over and stood beside Tucker. Tucker put his arm around the boy's shoulder. "Ellisandra Cooper, with Jack's permission I would like to ask you to be my wife. Jack, can I marry your mom?"

"Okay," Jack said and then ran back to his toys.

Tears fell heavily and Ellie remained silent as Tucker took out a ring box from his pants pocket, opened the box, and revealed a sparkling solitaire diamond ring.

"Oh, Tucker, it's beautiful," she told him, but not holding out her hand to receive it.

Tucker looked uneasy believing he had perhaps made a mistake asking her to marry him so soon.

"Tucker, you're right; everything is moving so quickly. It's like a tornado swept through and brought us to this point in a matter of a few months." She stopped talking and grew silent, choosing instead to look at him and rub his hair. "But I don't care," she began again. "I don't care how short of a time it's been. I love you, too, Tucker Adelson, and I would like nothing more than to be your wife." She extended her hand so he could put the diamond on her finger.

Tucker stood and they kissed while her aunt and uncle

got up and they had a group hug.

"I'm going to do everything in my power to make you and Jack happy," Tucker told her.

"I'm so glad you opened your heart this Christmas," her aunt said, "because the real gift was that you found love still lived inside."

The End

Words from the Author

In *The House Husband*, Ellie Cooper shut down her heart and closed the door on loving again because of grief. Grief presents itself by exhibiting many faces. There can be the type of grief you experience over losing a job. There is grief you experience over leaving a home that you've lived in all of your childhood, and now you find yourself moving into your own place. There can be the grief you experience as your children become adults and move out of the house, leaving you all alone. However, there is a grief that surpasses all of the above; and that is the grief of losing a loved one through death. When we lose a loved one, the holidays can be exceptionally hard, especially during the first few years and sometimes forever.

I want to tell you, and it's only because of my own personal experiences throughout life that I can say this—do not let the events, situations, and occurrences in your life make you bitter toward God. Many times we experience trying times in life that make us question the reason God allows things to happen. We may not always know why He does what He does. We may not always understand why He allows what He allows, but we can rest assured that He does absolutely nothing without a reason and a purpose, nor without turning the situation around to work for our good. God's plans for us are not to harm us, but to prosper us so we can have a future and a hope. He loves us and although we may not understand it all, His Word says that we should not lean to our own understanding. We should acknowledge God as being God and He will direct our paths. God will take care of You! I guarantee it!

Thank you for reading another book by Shelia E. Bell

Contact information
www.sheliaebell.net
www.sheliawritesbooks.com
sheliawritesbooks@yahoo.com
www.facebook.com/sheliawritesbooks
@sheliaebell (Twitter & Instagram)
@literacyrocks (Instagram)

Please join my mailing list for literary updates and
new book release information
www.sheliawritesbooks.com

If you enjoyed this book (or even if you did not) please
go to your favorite review site and leave a review!

This is My Confession

My name is Shelia E. Bell. I confess that
I am a writer.
I am a nationally renowned bestselling author.
I am God's amazing girl.
I confess that I write perfect stores about imperfect
people
Like Me *and* Like YOU!

Thanks for reading another book by Shelia E. Bell!

www.ingramcontent.com/pod-product-compliance
Lightning Source LLC
Chambersburg PA
CBHW052013170626
46808CB00007B/2904